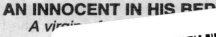

A self-confessed romance junkie, **INDIA GREY** was just thirteen years old when she first sent off for Harlequin's writers' guidelines. She can still recall the thrill of getting the large brown envelope with its distinctive logo through the letter box, and subsequently whiling away many a dull school day staring out of the window and dreaming of the perfect hero. She kept these guidelines with her for the next ten years, tucking them carefully inside the cover of each new diary in January, and beginning every list of New Year's resolutions with the words Start Novel. In the meantime, she also gained a degree in English literature and language from Manchester University, and in a stroke of genius on the part of the Gods of Romance, met her gorgeous future husband on the very last night of their three years there. The past fifteen years have been spent blissfully buried in domesticity and heaps of pink washing, generated by three small daughters, but she has never really stopped daydreaming about romance. She's just profoundly grateful to have finally got an excuse to do it legitimately!

ANGELO'S CAPTIVE VIRGIN
INDIA GREY

~ AN INNOCENT IN HIS BED ~

TORONTO • NEW YORK • LONDON
AMSTERDAM • PARIS • SYDNEY • HAMBURG
STOCKHOLM • ATHENS • TOKYO • MILAN • MADRID
PRAGUE • WARSAW • BUDAPEST • AUCKLAND

ISBN-13: 978-0-373-82370-3
ISBN-10:   0-373-82370-3

ANGELO'S CAPTIVE VIRGIN

First North American Publication 2008.

Previously published in the U.K. under the title
THE ITALIAN'S CAPTIVE VIRGIN

www.eHarlequin.com

Printed in U.S.A.

ANGELO'S CAPTIVE VIRGIN

To John. Thank you for the Happy Ever After.

PROLOGUE

THE dress was ivory satin, heavy and smooth. Once a nineteen-fifties cocktail dress belonging to Grandmère, Anna's mother had taken it in to fit Anna's skinny ten-year-old frame and added a narrow grosgrain ribbon around the waist, just above where the skirt flared out with wonderful fullness. An old piece of net curtain trimmed with tiny crystal beads and fixed down with a pleasingly authentic-looking plastic tiara completed the picture.

'It's beautiful.' Anna looked at herself in the mirror, her dark eyes shining with joy. 'Just like what a real bride would wear. It's the best birthday present ever. Thank you, Mama.'

Lisette smiled. 'Happy Birthday, *chérie. You're* beautiful. You look like a fairy princess.'

Anna frowned. She knew it wasn't true. Fairy princesses would be soft and blonde and blue-eyed like her mother, not olive-skinned and dark like she was. But she loved the dress all the same.

She was lucky that her birthday always fell in the summer holidays, when she and her mother were staying with Grandmère at Château Belle-Eden, and that summer she did nothing but play weddings. Gathering armfuls of flowers from the château's garden, she entwined garlands of jasmine and ivy around the banisters and tied heavy old-fashioned roses into spiky bouquets. In the hot, still afternoons the hallway was cool and the dim light filtering through the magnificent stained-glass dome above cast shimmering patterns on to the pale stone floor. While her mother played the piano in the salon Anna would drift down the stairs, shedding petals from her wilting rose bouquet, towards her imaginary waiting groom.

She pictured him standing at the bottom of the sweeping staircase, looking exactly like the prince in her book of fairy tales. Tall, blond, impossibly elegant in his morning coat, she imagined over and over again the moment when he would turn and look up at her.

The love that blazed in his blue eyes took her breath away every time.

CHAPTER ONE

'*C'EST tout, mademoiselle?*'

Anna cast a last look at her childhood, jumbled into the back of the auctioneer's van, and swallowed hard.

'Yes. That's all.'

The man slid up the tailgate and dusted off his big hands. '*Bien, mademoiselle.* There are just a few boxes left in the attic now; nothing that can go in a Paris saleroom, I'm afraid. Perhaps a local firm, a *brocante*?

Anna nodded, absent-mindedly scuffing the dusty gravel with the toe of her little green ballet pump, then stopping abruptly. She'd spent too long in tatty espadrilles hanging around with the GreenPlanet gang—she'd almost forgotten how to behave in proper clothes.

She straightened up and smiled apologetically at the removal man. His face softened. He'd worked for Paris's top auction house for a good many years now, so by rights nothing should surprise him any more. Aristocrats were an eccentric lot, and English aristocrats were the oddest of all, but Lady Roseanna Delafield was like no one he had ever come across before. With her silky black hair shot through with pink streaks and her quick, graceful ballerina's movements, she was like a pedigree kitten who had got lost and gone feral. Today her hair was caught back in a discreet knot at the nape of her neck, she was wearing a little black linen shift dress that made her skin glow like sun-kissed apricots and she looked for all the world like any other smart young lady of breeding, but nothing could quite disguise the vulnerability in those big dark eyes.

'*Bon chance, ma petite*,' he said kindly, climbing into the driver's seat of his lorry. 'Is sad to say goodbye to somewhere where we 'ave been 'appy, no?'

Anna shrugged sadly. 'Yes. But maybe it's not goodbye just yet. You never know…'

Leaning out of the window the man laughed. 'Miracles do 'appen, *chérie*. I 'ope you find one.' He started the engine and winked at her. 'You deserve it. *Au revoir*.'

Anna watched the van disappear round the bend in the drive, through the pine trees, then she turned and walked slowly back into the château. Inside the hot, late summer air was heavy with the smell of decay and her eyes travelled desolately around the once-splendid entrance hall. The duck-egg-blue silk that lined the walls was rotting and torn; pale squares were left where the men had taken down the paintings and darker patches showed the ravages of damp.

Her little low-heeled shoes echoed on the leaf-strewn floor as she walked slowly up the stairs. Above her, miraculously the stained glass dome was still intact and at that moment a shaft of afternoon sunlight sent shimmering pools of light on to the stairs. She smiled, remembering how she used to love trying to catch those rippling rainbows as a child, and how they used to fall in vivid splashes on the white bride's dress she'd got for her birthday that summer when she'd played the wedding game.

That last summer before her mother had died.

She jumped as her mobile phone rang, and slid it out of her bag.

'Fliss, I'm on my way. The auctioneer people just left, so I'm just going to lock up and leave.'

'OK, honey, I'll order you a very strong Martini.' Fliss's

voice was warm with compassion and understanding. 'Are you getting the bus?'

'No. One of the guys in the GreenPlanet camp has a bike I can borrow. It's only a few miles.'

From the other end of the phone Fliss gave a snort of laughter. 'You're joking, right? Anna, *no one* has ever arrived at the Hotel Paradis *by bike*. Are you going to get it valet parked?'

Stamping up a narrower flight of stairs to the attic, Anna scowled. 'Don't be silly. I don't see why I should pump carbon monoxide into the atmosphere just to keep the parking valets at the Paradis in tips.'

'OK, OK, spare me the environmental lecture.' The laughter died in Fliss's voice, leaving her sounding suddenly subdued. 'Talking of which, how's life in the GreenPlanet camp? Have you finished saving the world for the rest of us yet?'

Anna wandered over to the forlorn stack of boxes and old trunks the men had left piled in the middle of the dusty attic. 'We're still working on it,' she said stiffly, lifting the lid of a metal-banded trunk at her feet and finding herself looking down at a jumble of old clothes. 'Saving Château Belle-Eden from this…this vile property developer would be a good start, though.'

'Well, if word in our office is correct and the "vile property developer" in question *is* Angelo Emiliani you don't stand a cat in hell's chance of saving it,' Fliss retorted, then, hearing Anna's soft gasp, said, 'Anna? What's the matter?'

'Nothing. I've just found my old dressing-up box. All my ballet stuff is in here—my first pointe shoes.' Reverently she wound the trailing ribbons around the tattered slippers, then slowly pulled out a crushed tumble of heavy cream satin from the depths of the trunk. 'The wedding dress!'

Anna held the dress out at arm's length, gazing wonderingly at it. She'd thought it was so perfect, but now she could see how home-made it looked, how obvious that it had been inexpertly cut down from one of Grandmère's gowns and trimmed with mismatched bits salvaged from other garments. The fabric had yellowed with age and was spotted with mildew in places. Wedging the phone against her shoulder, she held the dress up against her and twirled slowly around.

'To think I truly believed *this* made me look like a real bride,' she said vaguely. 'A fairy princess… I must have been spectacularly naïve…'

That was an understatement.

Abruptly she tore the dress away from her body and dropped it back into the box. 'Anyway,' she continued briskly, 'like I said, there's nothing left for me to do here. I'm on my way.'

'Great. I'll be in the terrace bar, provided we can get a table. Don't forget it's Saskia Middleton's twenty-first tonight too, so wear something suitable. You *are* wearing something suitable, aren't you?' Fliss added, sounding worried. 'Only I haven't quite got over the puffball-skirt-and-biker-boots combo from Lucinda's party at Christmas. Her poor mother didn't know what to say.'

Anna glanced down at the subdued black dress. 'Don't panic, I'm looking deeply respectable,' she said ruefully. 'And it's entirely in your honour, as I have absolutely no intention of going to Saskia Middleton's party. I'd rather spend an evening with Lucretia Borgia and Hannibal Lecter. But go and grab a table on the terrace and get those Martinis ordered. I'll be there in fifteen minutes.'

Hanging up before Fliss could argue about the party, Anna turned back to the wedding dress, stroking her hand over the slippery satin.

How much had changed since that long ago summer, when she had thought that life was simple.

Nothing was simple. Nothing was what she'd thought it was.

Herself included.

The château was just about all that was left of that old life. And that, she thought fiercely, standing up and walking quickly across the room and down the stairs, was why she had no intention of letting it go without a fight. It was nothing whatsoever to do with any lingering fantasies about white dresses and wedding bells, but her mother was dead, her dreams were broken, her own sense of who she was shaken to the core. *That* was why she had to hang on to the last shreds of the person she used to think she was.

A door slammed below.

Crossing the landing, Anna stopped dead. A little gust of air seemed to shiver through the building, then everything sank back into stillness. But the atmosphere had changed. There was a charge in the air, like electricity before a storm, and with a pulse of horrified certainty Anna knew she was no longer alone in the house.

She froze and then, with agonizing caution, tiptoed to the top of the stairs.

For a long moment there was no sound at all.

Then, with a mounting sense of panic, she heard footsteps moving across the hall. Instinctively she recognized them as male: slow, measured and sounding like the footsteps of the axe-murderer in every horror film she'd ever seen.

The footsteps stopped.

Forcing herself to lean forward, she tentatively peered over the banisters, then drew back with a sharp intake of breath.

She was right.

He was male. Very male. And very blond. Perhaps it was just because she was looking down on him from directly above that he seemed to have the broadest shoulders she'd ever seen.

'Hello?'

His voice was deep and faintly accented. He didn't sound like a murderer. He sounded gorgeous. Anna swallowed. The ability to speak had inexplicably deserted her, but the pounding of her heart seemed to echo through the whole building, declaring her presence with every beat.

'Who's there?'

She opened her mouth but the only sound that came out was a dry croak.

There was a muttered curse from below. 'All right then, I'll come up.'

Oh, God. She was being utterly ridiculous and in a moment he—whoever he was—was going to come up and see her cowering on the landing like some frightened animal. Drawing herself up to her full five foot three inches, she smoothed down the slightly creased linen of her dress. 'Don't bother,' she called, clenching her fists into balls of determination and desperately trying to assume an air of insouciance. She moved to the top of the stairs and began to descend.

Halfway down she steeled herself to glance down at him and had to grip the banister to stop herself from falling. There was a roaring of blood in her ears and a dizzying surge of adrenalin flooded her body.

The man who stood at the foot of the stairs was her fantasy made flesh. For a moment time seemed to stand still and the years melt away, until she could have easily believed that she was ten years old again, a ragged bouquet of forget-me-nots and roses clasped in her hands, sweeping down the stairs to meet her hero. He was there, just as she had imagined him so many times.

Only his silver-blue eyes weren't filled with adoration.

They were icy cold.

'*Gesù*, who the hell are you?'

Angelo Emiliani was aware of the hostility in his tone and didn't bother to try and disguise it.

Arundel-Ducasse may be one of the longest established estate agents in the business, with offices in all the major European cities, but in his dealings with them over the past couple of weeks they had hardly stunned him with their efficiency. Now it seemed they'd not only got the time of his appointment wrong, so thwarting his plan to look around the château on his own first, but they'd also sent some juvenile delinquent office girl.

And, unfortunately for her, patience was not his strong point.

She stopped on the third step from the bottom, where her eyes were just about level with his, looking both nervous and defiant. In spite of his irritation, Angelo felt a vague, instinctive stirring inside him.

'Maybe I should ask you the same question,' she snapped.

'Oh, dear.' His tone was languid and mocking as he turned and walked into the centre of the hallway, his eyes travelling speculatively around the room. 'Am I to assume that the entire Nice office of Arundel-Ducasse have been struck down with the Black Death or something equally debilitating? I cannot imagine any other circumstances in which it would be necessary to send the girl who does the photocopying on a major viewing such as this.'

Behind him she gave a little gasp.

'Angelo Emiliani.'

Something in her voice jolted him out of his preoccupied irritation and he glanced sharply at her, noticing her properly for the first time.

At first he had assumed that the rainbow streaks in her hair were caused by the light from the stained-glass dome above them, but now he could see that there were indeed jagged blazes of shocking pink beneath the dark silk that was drawn back from her delicate heart-shaped face. His gaze travelled over her slowly, taking in the smoky kohl-rimmed eyes and the short black dress, the oddly defiant set of her small chin. Realization slotted into his brain like a well-oiled bolt sliding home. Of course. He'd spotted the protesters' camp through the trees as he'd approached the château. He gave a slow smile.

'Correct, *signorina*. And your name is…?'

Her hesitation was almost unnoticeable, then, with a little jangle of silver bracelets, she thrust out a slender hand and spoke in confident cut-glass tones.

'Forgive me, Signor Emiliani, you caught me off guard. I'm Felicity from the London office of Arundel-Ducasse. I've been liaising with the Marquess of Ifford over the sale of the château. I'm on holiday in Cannes, so I thought I'd come and see it for myself.'

That was pretty quick thinking. He had to hand it to her—she was a vast improvement on the usual spotty, dreadlocked eco-warriors that picketed his development sites and protested outside his offices in Rome and London.

'I see.' He looked down at the grimy limestone floor and tried to suppress a smile. Protester-baiting was one of his favourite sports and this time there was an added piquancy thanks to the unprecedented lusciousness of the quarry. The urge to play along with her little charade was irresistible. 'Well, I'm very glad that you did, Felicity.' He took a step towards her and watched with satisfaction as a shadow passed across her extraordinary wide-set eyes. 'Very glad indeed. As you'll have gathered, your colleague from the far less efficient Nice office hasn't appeared and due to unwelcome...*developments*...I'm very keen to get this deal sorted out today.'

'Developments?'

He sighed. 'Our little group of campers in the woods. I saw them as I came up the drive and the sooner my name is on the deeds for this property, the sooner I can send them on their way to spend their time doing something worthwhile. I hate to see idealistic young people wasting their time on a lost cause.'

Anna clenched her fists so that the fingernails dug painfully into her palms. Until this moment she wouldn't honestly have been able to list 'self-control' as being one of her personal strong points, but it seemed she certainly had more of it than she thought. How else was she managing to restrain herself from throwing herself at Angelo hot-shot Emiliani and raking her nails down his arrogant, self-satisfied, obscenely handsome face?

He took a step towards her, his eyes fixed on hers. 'So it's your lucky day, Felicity. As you'll be the one to show me the property, you'll be the one who gets the commission on the sale.'

Anna felt the blood drain from her face. She felt like Judas taking his thirty pieces of silver. The thought of walking through each familiar room of her beloved château in the company of the man who intended to take it from her made her feel dizzy with horror.

He was still looking at her, his narrow blue eyes glittering with ice.

'That won't be a problem, will it, *signorina*? You *are* an employee of the estate agency that is supposed to be selling this property, are you not?'

'Yes, of course, as I said I…'

'Good. And you said you've been handling its marketing in the London office, in which case you should know your way around?'

She met his gaze with a steadiness that surprised him. 'Yes.'

'Then let's not waste any more time.' He smiled suddenly and it lit up his exquisite features and carved perfectly symmetrical brackets on each side of his generous mouth. 'I've scheduled the first of my contractors to be on site here next week, so as you can see I can't afford to hang around.'

'Isn't that a little presumptuous? Until the contracts are signed, nothing is certain.'

'Not presumptuous. Realistic. I always get what I want. Now, are you going to show me around or do I have to phone the Nice office and get someone out here who knows what they're doing?'

She looked up at him and gave him her sweetest smile.

'Where would you like to start?'

His eyes flickered downwards for a second, causing her stomach to tighten convulsively and a gasp to rise in her throat.

'How about the master bedroom?'

Breathe in… Hold… And out…

It was no good. The surge of white-hot tingling fury that was currently coursing through her veins wasn't going to be calmed down with yoga. She needed tranquillisers at the very least. Or a general anaesthetic.

The trouble was, she admitted disgustedly to herself, it wasn't just anger that was making her knees shake so much that she had to lean on the banisters for support. Waiting on the landing outside what used to be her grandmother's room, Anna cursed her own stupidity and the pathetic weakness that had made her hormones sing in response to his blatant flirting.

How could she have told such a ridiculous lie? Fliss would kill her when she found out she had 'borrowed' her identity. Oh, God—supposing Emiliani complained to her boss and she got into terrible trouble? Anna felt panic surge through her.

She'd just have to be very, very nice to the obnoxious Signor Emiliani and make sure that he had no cause to complain, but jeez, that wasn't going to be easy. How could he be so complacent—so sure of himself—to have already scheduled contractors to start destroying her beloved château when the sale was far from assured? She felt a fresh wave of indignation crash through her at the thought.

Thank goodness for GreenPlanet. It wasn't over yet.

She turned. Through the open doorway she could see him standing at the window. He was leaning against the sill, his arms stretched out on either side and his broad shoulders blocking out an unreasonable amount of daylight. No doubt he was planning which parts of the formal parterre would have to be flattened to make way for the helipad and all-weather tennis courts, she thought bitterly, trying not to notice the way his unruly blond hair curled on to the collar of his dark linen suit, or the length of the suntanned fingers resting so lightly on the window sill. Even with his back to her there was something about his slim-hipped, elegant figure that screamed self-assurance and power.

I always get what I want.

GreenPlanet was no match for him, she acknowledged with

a mixture of despair and awful, treacherous excitement. He had an aura of quiet, dangerous focus that made her shiver.

Levering himself upright, he turned to her and she experienced a momentary *frisson* of shock at the youthful beauty of his face. The skin over his elegant cheekbones was taut and bronzed, and his aura of restless energy was like that of an exotic animal in the absolute peak of physical condition. He couldn't be that much older than she was and yet he seemed as hard and cold and jaded as a man twice his age. What the hell had happened to turn him to stone?

'Well?'

'Well what?' she stuttered, suddenly jolted out of her thoughts and aware that she'd been staring. Although he was no doubt used to that.

He leaned his narrow hips against the window sill and folded his arms. 'Come on, Felicity, you can do better than that. This is the part where you're supposed to talk about location and square footage and security. You're an *estate agent*, remember?'

His voice was quiet, amused, slightly reproving. Anna gritted her teeth as she recognized that he was testing her, teasing her.

'Of course. And you're an internationally renowned property developer, *signor*,' she retorted, trying to keep her tone light. 'I wouldn't presume to tell you anything about this building or any other, since of the two of us you are so clearly the expert.'

'Wouldn't or couldn't?'

He spoke very softly, the words dropping into the silence like pebbles into a lake. Anna felt the ripples spreading through the still air between them and, despite the warmth of the afternoon, she shivered suddenly.

He was *so* on to her. And so enjoying it. For the sake of her own pride as well as Fliss's professional reputation, she had to do a bit better than this.

'What do you want to know?' Squaring her shoulders, she walked slowly towards him, slipping again into that clipped upper-crust drawl. 'As I'm sure you can see for yourself, Château Belle-Eden is a perfect example of the nineteenth century Anglo-Norman style, set in five acres of prime real estate in one of the world's most desirable locations.'

'Very impressive.'

'That was the intention.' She had reached the window now and stood beside him, unable to meet his eyes. 'It was built in 1897 for the owner of one of Paris's most exclusive department stores and no expense was spared on its construction or its furnishings. The walls were covered with silk from—'

'I wasn't actually talking about the property.'

'I beg your pardon?'

He was looking at her steadily. 'I was referring to your in-depth knowledge of Château Belle-Eden.'

'I told you, I've been responsible for the marketing of this property at the London end,' she said abruptly, staring straight ahead of her to where the driveway snaked through the pine trees towards the road and the cliffs beyond. 'As I was saying, this is one of the most sought after locations in the world. Cannes is a mere three kilometres away, the château has its own stretch of private beach, accessed through the pine forest—which you can see over there to your left.'

'Ah, yes.' Much to Anna's relief, he shifted his smoky, searching gaze and looked out of the window to where the GreenPlanet tents and guy-ropes of washing were just about visible above the pine trees. His eyes were narrowed and slightly menacing.

'Do you intend to keep the château as a private residence, Signor Emiliani?' she asked, trying to keep her tone casual.

Slowly he turned back to face her with a mocking smile. 'No. I thought I'd use it as a youth hostel. And maybe establish a permanent camp over there in the woods for hippies and drop-outs. That way maybe I'd be able to get on with my other projects at least without having them constantly on my case.'

She didn't flinch, he noticed. Not a flicker of emotion passed through those slanting, watchful eyes.

'It was a genuine enquiry, *signor.*'

'I'm sure it was. But if you think I'd be stupid enough to tell you honestly what I plan to do with this building then you're obviously underestimating me.'

She looked steadily at him. 'Have you finished here?'

There it was again. She was perfectly polite, perfectly correct, but he picked up that tiny spark of challenge which a man who was less in tune with his instincts would undoubtedly have missed. Angelo Emiliani had not come from an orphanage in Milan to take his place in the international rich lists by behaving as other men did. Instinct was his speciality.

'For the time being, yes.'

'Good. Follow me.'

'My pleasure.'

And it certainly was a pleasure, he thought idly, watching the way the short linen dress cast undulating shadows on to the backs of her slim brown thighs as she sauntered down corridors, opening the doors on an endless succession of vast empty rooms. Despite the perfect respectability of the dress, there was something oddly rebellious about the way she wore it. Maybe it was the way she had teamed it with those slim bangles which made a soft, silvery, musical sound as she moved, or maybe it was the contrast of her long golden legs beneath the sober black.

There was something about this girl that whispered *'toxic'*. She gave the impression that the lightest brush against her would result in chemical burns.

The fact that she was lying to him didn't disturb Angelo at all. The fact that she was doing it so convincingly bothered him a little more. Environmental protesters were a constant source of irritation and disruption in his business, but he had never considered them to be a serious threat to his plans before. But this girl knew more about this property than a hippy-dippy eco-warrior should do.

It didn't cross his mind for a second that he might be wrong about her. So what if she had the diction of a minor royal and the lithe movements of a dancer? She was no more some posh airhead office girl than he was. It wasn't just the pink streaks in her hair that gave her away, but the hostility that crackled around her like static. She might as well have had 'REBEL' tattooed on to her skin in inch-high letters.

Maybe she did. Somewhere.

Desire hit him like the lash of a whip, sudden and stinging.

'In here is a slightly smaller bedroom, but the view of the sea more than makes up for the less sizable proportions...' She spoke before she'd opened the door, he noticed, but, walking into the room, Angelo's eyes narrowed as he ascertained that what she had just said was completely spot on.

He felt a cold pulse of adrenalin rush through him along with the realization that the group she belonged to may have some rich benefactor who was planning to put in a rival bid for the château. It wasn't such a ridiculous idea. There were plenty of stratospherically wealthy Hollywood celebs who would be only too willing to toss a few million in the direction of an environmental charity—especially if it meant acquiring such a gem of a property at the same time as making them feel they were doing their bit to save the planet. With the exception of the charity involved, it wasn't so very different from what he planned to do with it. And the prospect of having those plans thwarted by a group of tree-huggers was unthinkable.

In the past he had bought properties out of boredom or for a challenge or simply to irritate the people who tried to stop him, but this one was different. Angelo Emiliani wasn't in the habit of analyzing his feelings—in fact his entire purpose in life was to keep busy enough to avoid having to have them at all—but he was prepared to acknowledge how much this project mattered to him. For old times' sake.

For Lucia.

'…south facing, meaning the light is particularly lovely in here.'

There was something wistful in her tone that jerked him back to the present. Thrusting his hands into his pockets, he took a steadying breath in before turning his attention back to her.

She was standing by the window, looking out across the treetops to where the sea lay in a glittering arc. And she was right about the light, he thought bitterly. The evening sun fell on to her face, outlining her profile in gold-dust, highlighting the sudden softness of her sulky mouth. Crushing down the anger that smouldered somewhere inside his chest, he managed a smile.

'You've been very helpful, Felicity. Really. I appreciate you showing me round.'

She looked up at him and blinked, clearly taken by surprise by the softness of his tone. Walking slowly towards her, he could see that she was trembling slightly, but bravado flashed in her dark eyes. The combination caused an odd sensation in the pit of his stomach, which he recognized as lust spiked with something more complicated.

'It's nothing. I shouldn't have been here really…'

He stopped a couple of feet away from her. 'I'm very glad you were. I'll be sure to tell your boss how impressed I am by your professional dedication.'

That shook her. He tried not to let the tiny leap of triumph in his chest show on his face as he watched the colour flood her cheeks.

'Please don't. I probably shouldn't have—'

The bare room was bathed in softest apricot, turning the pink in her hair to gleaming copper.

'OK—but let me make it up to you in some other way. You said you were staying in Cannes—please let me take you out for dinner tonight.'

'I can't,' she said hastily. 'I'm meeting a friend.' She glanced at her watch. 'In fact, I'm late. I really should go.'

He nodded. Her refusal didn't surprise him in the slightest—he hadn't expected anything else—but, looking at those slanting, wary, kohl-smudged eyes, he felt a sharp kick of disappointment which caught him completely unawares.

She was already walking to the door, casting a last look around the room before going out on to the landing.

He followed her. Her footsteps echoed on the wooden stairs as she ran down them.

'Where are you staying? I'll give you a lift.'

Smiling slightly, he wondered how she would get out of that one, but she tossed a nonchalant glance at him over her shoulder.

'Thanks. Hotel Paradis, if that's not out of your way?'

Watching her shut the front door of the château, Angelo felt himself frowning.

He was used to having all the answers, to being at least ten steps ahead of the game. But he had to admit it that right now this girl had him floundering in the dark.

Which was an intoxicating image. But a very disturbing feeling.

CHAPTER TWO

'NICE car.'

Anna made an effort to mask her contempt behind a façade of admiration as she glanced around the white leather interior of the ridiculously flashy sports car. But she couldn't quite stop herself from adding with a simper, 'I always think that cars say so much about their owners.'

This one was shouting, *I belong to a man with obscene amounts of cash and issues about his masculinity*, she thought with some satisfaction. Maybe Angelo Emiliani wasn't as cool as he came across.

'Do you?'

Admittedly his voice was infuriatingly cool, as was the way he seemed to lounge in the driver's seat, controlling the powerful car with one hand and easing it around hairpin bends on the narrow road at speeds which…

Anna swallowed and averted her eyes from the speedometer.

'So you've no doubt come to the conclusion that I'm an insecure misogynist with more money than taste?' She felt the colour leap to her cheeks at the accuracy of his guess. 'Well, I hate to spoil the theory, but the car is only hired. I simply asked for the fastest model available—which should tell you that I'm very impatient and I like to get everything done in the shortest possible time.'

'In that case, wouldn't it make more sense to have a chauffeur? So you don't need to lose a second of valuable working time?'

'Yes. But my impatience is perhaps only outweighed by my desire for control.' His mouth curved into the merest suggestion of an ironic smile, letting her know he'd picked up the minute sting of sarcasm in her tone, and his blue gaze flickered over her for a second. A blissful, spine-tingling second. 'I do have a chauffeur, of course. But wherever practical I prefer to drive myself. What about you, *signorina*? What sort of car do you drive?'

'I don't. Cars are—'

She was about to spring automatically into the standard GreenPlanet sermon about the evils wrought on the planet by the internal combustion engine, but managed to stop herself just in time. Not, however, before she noticed the smirk of satisfaction on Angelo Emiliani's face.

'A nuisance where I live, in Central London,' she finished lamely, looking out of the window. 'I take the tube everywhere.'

He'd very nearly caught her out. And, dammit, he knew it. He didn't reply, but his silence spoke more articulately than anything he could have said.

The traffic grew heavier as they came into Cannes, and Angelo guided the car effortlessly through the streams of expensive vehicles towards the hotel. He wondered what she would do when they got there. Wait until he had gone and hitch a lift back to the protesters' camp, he guessed. There was no way she could possibly be telling the truth about staying at the Paradis.

Was there?

'I don't think I got your full name,' he said casually. With this girl it was best not to take any chances.

'Hanson-Brooks'

'Felicity Hanson-Brooks,' he repeated, echoing her clipped upper-class pronunciation with a slight curl of his lip. That accent, with its suggestion of effortless privilege and complacency, never failed to set his teeth on edge and make his hackles rise. 'That's a very smart name.'

She glanced across at him and shrugged slightly. Defensively?

Out of the corner of his eye he watched her stretch out her long legs and shift slightly in her seat, arching her back away from the hot leather upholstery with the lissom grace of a cat stretching.

Angelo Emiliani had slept with so many women—from cocktail waitresses to *contessas*. Novelty, the ruthless pursuit of the new, which was what drove him in his work, was something he no longer expected to experience in the bedroom.

But he'd never had an eco-warrior.

Idly he wondered what lay beneath that perfectly simple, perfectly demure black linen dress. There was something raw about her, something earthy. He had grown tired of the neat, waxed sterility that turned every woman he undressed into a conveyor-belt Barbie—perfect and plastic. This girl looked as if she was liberatingly, excitingly beyond all of that. He breathed in deeply, savouring the thought, and was suddenly aware of the scent of her.

She smelled of dark things—bitter chocolate, black coffee, overlaid with woodsmoke.

Strong. Exotic. Delicious.

Benedetto Gesù. The very things he didn't trust about her were the things that turned him on.

He swung into the hotel's VIP forecourt more recklessly than he had intended and brought the car to a halt in a screech of brakes. For a moment neither of them moved and the interior of the small car suddenly seemed thick with swirling undercurrents of meaning.

His hand, still on the handbrake, was inches from her bare thigh. He flexed his fingers around the brake, and then was instantly, uncomfortably aware of the phallic symbolism of the gesture.

And so was she.

Slowly her eyes travelled upwards, until she was looking at him from beneath her lashes as shaming colour rushed to her cheeks. He must have guessed what she was thinking, he must be mocking her, she thought in miserable humiliation. How amusingly predictable that she should end up falling under his spell like every other woman. Groping for the door handle, she mustered what she hoped was a cool smile, but her attempt at nonchalance was totally ruined by the fact that she couldn't work out how to open the door.

He leaned across her and she flattened herself against the back of the seat to avoid coming into contact with the hard length of his body. But she could smell his cool, clean scent. He straightened up slowly and she scrambled out of the car.

'Thanks for the lift, Signor Emiliani.'

He nodded curtly, suddenly finding that the acerbic retort he would usually have found eluded him. For a fraction of a second there he had been out of control—of the car and of his ruthlessly contained emotions—and the realisation had left a very bitter taste in his mouth.

He should follow her, he thought savagely as he watched her run lightly up the steps to the hotel, but the tell-tale evidence of her effect on him made movement temporarily inadvisable. Slamming his fist down on the steering wheel, he waited a moment, then got stiffly out of the low driving seat and leaned against the roof of the car, watching her all the time.

At the top of the steps she paused and turned her head towards the long rows of little metal tables that spilled out from the hotel's ultra-fashionable bar on to a balcony overlooking the beach. At this hour of the early evening they were already crowded with those who were wealthy and well-connected enough to be able to afford to drink in one of the most exclusive watering holes on the Riviera, and beautiful enough to want to be seen there.

Angelo's eyes narrowed as he watched her wave frantically before hurrying inside. He straightened up, searching the crowd on the outdoor terrace for the person she could have been greeting, but in the crush of lithe, designer-clad bodies perched at tables and standing in groups it was impossible to distinguish anyone in particular.

Which, he thought savagely, tossing the car keys to a uniformed concierge, was exactly what she had calculated. It was all part of the game she was playing to try to persuade him that she genuinely was some harmless, well-bred English girl, holidaying on the Riviera with a similarly respectable friend.

He didn't intend to let her get away with it.

Ignoring the polite greeting of the doorman, he stalked angrily through the opulent lobby to the reception desk. While he waited his eyes roved restlessly over the shifting groups of people, but there was no sign of her.

The blonde receptionist batted thickly mascaraed eyelashes at him as he asked for Felicity Hanson-Brooks's room number.

'Well, *monsieur*, we're really not supposed to…'

'Please. She gave it to me last night and I arranged to pick her up, but I'm afraid I've forgotten it.' He gave her his most helpless smile and watched her melt. 'I can't stand her up.'

Blushing furiously under her heavy make-up, the girl gave it to him and was rewarded with a smile that would give her sleepless nights for the next month.

His face hardening as he turned away, Angelo took a seat on a Louis XIV-style sofa beneath a hideous golden palm tree and thoughtfully took out his phone. That hadn't been the outcome he had expected. He checked his watch. It was too late now to catch any of his contacts in the London office of Arundel-Ducasse, and he was starting to get a nasty feeling that he might just be in for a surprise there too.

Was his instinct about this girl completely wrong?

With fresh determination he speed-dialled his PA and asked

her to arrange for his chauffeur to bring his dinner suit down to the Paradis. He wasn't leaving tonight until he'd got some answers. In the meantime, he had a deal to finalise.

'OK, you have precisely thirty seconds to explain.'

Leaning over the little table, Anna gave Fliss a brief hug then sank down into one of the trendy aluminium chairs and took a long sip of the drink that was waiting for her.

''Splain wha'?' she queried innocently around the ridiculous straw and cocktail olive with which the Hotel Paradis saw fit to furnish their Martinis. The ice in hers had melted long ago so it was warm and watery, but it still had a very welcome alcoholic kick.

Leaning back in her seat, Fliss tapped her foot and tried to look cross, but her eyes sparkled with excitement. 'Let me think now... Who invented cellulite? Why men don't have a shopping gene? Or maybe why you've turned up forty minutes late in the company of a gorgeous bloke?'

Sullenly Anna took a long suck of Martini. 'Hmm, that's actually quite interesting. You see "gorgeous bloke" and I see "ruthless, vulgar billionaire property developer."'

Fliss's eyes widened and she let out a long, low whistle.

'*That* was Angelo Emiliani?'

As reactions went it was a pretty satisfying one, Anna reflected sulkily, so why did it irritate the life out of her?

Fliss's eyes skimmed the terrace, as if hungry to see him again. 'Now I understand why the girls in our office call him The Ice Prince and fight each other practically to the death to take his calls. He is quite *amazingly* lush...'

Anna affected extreme indifference and looked into the distance, to where the sun was dyeing the surface of the sea the same colour as her hair.

'So the gossip was spot on,' Fliss mused eagerly. 'He's the mystery buyer for the château.'

'Correction,' snapped Anna. 'He's the *would-be* mystery buyer for the château. The papers aren't signed yet.'

Fliss glanced at her sharply. 'But they will be, surely? As soon as his offer is made formally? I mean, the whole point is that you and your father need the money from the sale, isn't it?'

Viciously Anna stabbed the olive with the cocktail stick. 'Of course. But I don't want to let Château Belle-Eden go to someone who's going to rip it apart and turn it into some hideous show-piece of trendy architecture.'

Fliss was looking at her steadily. 'And what about your father? What does he say about that?'

'Why should he care? He hasn't been near the place in years. He wouldn't care if Emiliani wanted to paint it purple and turn it into a vice den, but luckily, thanks to French inheritance law, it's half mine, so whatever he says the sale can't go ahead until I've signed the papers.'

'Right,' said Fliss decisively. 'I'll come with you if you like. You can introduce me to the delicious Signor Emiliani.'

Anna paled at the thought. As far as Angelo Emiliani was concerned he'd already met Felicity Hanson-Brooks, but now wasn't the time to confess about that. Not when Fliss had that scary look on her face.

'You *are* going to sign them, aren't you, Anna?'

Anna's gaze swept over the packed terrace. The setting sun gave the beautiful tanned faces of the Riviera crowd a flattering rosy glow. The noise of excited conversation was underlaid by a faint but insistent bass beat as the nightclubs and parties swung into life. Edgy and restless, Anna felt its feverish pulse echoed inside her.

'Eventually. I—that is, GreenPlanet too—just want to try to find out what he has in mind for it before the sale is completed. Gavin—one of the GreenPlanet guys—has heard something about a connection with a pharmaceutical company, and apparently Emiliani is intending to cut down most of the pine forest for a landing strip, which of course we're very concerned about. If that's the case—'

Fliss shook her glossy, well-groomed head. 'You won't stop him. The guy's legendary for making things happen. It's what he *does*. And hell, Anna, it's what he does *beautifully*. He'll make Belle-Eden into something wonderful.'

Seeing the stricken look on Anna's face, she realised instantly that she'd said the wrong thing. 'It's wonderful as it is,' Anna snapped. 'He can only ruin it. And the environment. All those trees—'

Fliss was looking at her steadily, sadly. 'Oh, Anna, that's not really the issue here, is it? Look, honey, I know when you had to give up ballet it hit you hard. It was your life, and it's left a big empty space which no one can blame you for trying to fill. But all this eco-stuff? Are you sure you really care about it enough to take on someone like Angelo Emiliani?'

Leaning her elbows on the table, Anna dropped her head into her hands. Suddenly she felt very tired. In the darkness behind her fingers the image of Angelo Emiliani standing at the window in her grandmother's room came back to her—tall, broad-shouldered and utterly sure of the power he wielded. His confidence was daunting.

It was also horribly, irresistibly attractive.

She felt Fliss's hand on her arm. 'Are you sure you're not just grasping at something to fill that empty space, and maybe—just maybe—get back at your father?'

Anna sat up abruptly and tugged out the band that held her hair back, letting it fall around her face with a flash of vivid pink.

'Oh, God, Fliss. Maybe. I don't know; I'm still so angry with him for not being honest with me for all those years. And with Mum, but that's awful because she's not here and I still miss her so much too. And that's why I can't just let go of the château. It's my last…link with her. It meant everything to her. It was a part of her.'

'I think you're wrong. It's just a place. She'd understand why it had to be sold. *You* meant everything to her. *You* were a part of her.'

Anna got stiffly to her feet and Fliss almost gasped at the pain in her eyes, still raw after all these years. 'Ah, but that's the thing, isn't it? I wasn't.' Clumsily she hitched her bag over her shoulder and pushed her chair in, then looked at Fliss with a bright, false smile. 'Anyway, you'd better go and get ready for Saskia's gruesome party.'

'Why don't you come?' Fliss was standing up too now, but beneath the red glow cast over the table by the umbrella her face was lined with concern. 'I know you hate her, but the party's in the nightclub downstairs; it'll be pitch dark and she'll have invited so many people you probably won't even see her.'

Anna smiled ruefully and began making her way through the crowd back to the hotel lobby. 'The GreenPlanet guys are having a party on the beach later on. I think I fit in better there somehow, don't you?'

'Who cares? You can fit in wherever you want to, Anna. Stop worrying about who you are or what you are and just relax.' Fliss was almost having to run to keep up with her, but that just meant she talked louder, her exasperated voice rising above the general chatter. Anna clenched her teeth and walked faster.

In the lobby she stopped, leaning against the trunk of a giant golden ornamental palm tree while she waited for Fliss to catch up. But a voice behind her caught her attention.

She felt her throat constrict, her stomach tighten as she recognised that deep, smooth timbre with its faint Italian accent.

She didn't even have to look round to know where he was. She could tell simply from seeing the direction in which the eyes of every woman in the room were drawn. But still she couldn't resist.

He was leaning against one of the ornamental palm trees also, his mobile phone pressed to his ear, his broad shoulders stooped and his blond head bent. Utterly self-contained, he looked languid and somehow separate from the bustle of the busy hotel. Only the staccato tap of one long brown finger on the golden tree trunk hinted at the restless energy beneath the impassive exterior.

She darted back out of sight behind her own palm tree, biting her lip, wishing as she used to when she was a little girl that she could click her heels like Dorothy in *The Wizard of Oz* and find herself back at home. If she left now he'd see her, and then he'd know that her story about staying in the hotel was a big lie. He'd probably find out sooner or later, but she wasn't ready to give him the satisfaction yet.

Fliss appeared and was just about to launch into reproach, but Anna pressed a finger to her lips. 'Listen, I'll come to the party,' she hissed urgently as Fliss looked at her in bewilderment. 'Can you lend me something to wear?'

Fliss nodded.

'Great. Thanks, Fliss. Now, we're going to walk quickly across this lobby to the lifts *without looking round*. Do you understand?'

Fliss nodded again, looking as if she thought there was a very real possibility that Anna was in fact seriously mentally disturbed. 'Why?'

'I'll tell you later. Let's go.'

Slowly, with admirable cool, she left the safety of her palm tree and sauntered past him, managing to keep her gaze firmly fixed ahead. Fliss, however, was much less disciplined and by the time she stepped into the lift her eyes were virtually out on stalks.

'It was him, wasn't it? Angelo Emiliani? He is *glorious*. I wonder if he's staying here.' She giggled. 'I wonder if I could find out his room number.'

But Anna wasn't listening. She was too busy thinking about the two words she'd just overheard Angelo Emiliani saying.

Words that, it would seem, proved that GreenPlanet were on the right lines.

Grafton-Tarrant.

The name of one of the biggest pharmaceutical companies in the world.

CHAPTER THREE

'BETTER?' asked Fliss with a grin as Anna emerged, pink-cheeked and wrapped in a towel, from her *en suite* bathroom.

'Much. The facilities in the Belle-Eden pinewoods aren't exactly five star,' Anna replied, vigorously towelling her hair. 'I've spent the last week hallucinating about hot baths and scented oils.'

Fliss opened the mini-bar and took out a couple of tiny bottles of Chablis. 'I'm so glad you decided to come tonight,' she said, unscrewing the tops and handing one to Anna before raising hers and taking a swig. 'Here's to Angelo Emiliani and whatever he did to make you change your mind.' Picking up a paperback and a bathrobe, she headed towards the bathroom and waved a hand airily around the room before she disappeared. 'Help yourself. Make-up, clothes, whatever—although I do have a dress in mind for you. I bought it because it was so lovely I couldn't leave it in the shop, but in all honesty it makes my boobs look like over-inflated balloons.'

'That's a bad thing?'

'Yep. Believe me. On you it'll look sensational.' Blowing a kiss, she vanished into the steam and shut the door.

Left alone, Anna sank on to the enormous bed and thought about what Fliss had just said.

Here's to Angelo Emiliani and whatever he did to make you change your mind.

But that was just it. He hadn't had to do anything. Just his presence down there in the lobby had been enough, and she had to admit that even his absence was pretty potent too. Throwing herself backwards on to the bed with a hungry moan, she gave in to the thoughts that had flitted distractingly though her head all evening, conjuring his face in her mind's eye, hearing the low rasp of his voice. Her body, still hot and damp from the bath, throbbed, reminding her of her forbidden feelings with devastating honesty. Trailing trembling, hesitant fingers down over her midriff, she imagined his touch…

There was a knock at the door.

Guiltily she snatched her hand away. Leaping up, she ran across the room, re-wrapping the towel tightly around herself and dragging a shaking hand through her damp hair. Breathlessly, aware of the blush creeping up her throat, she pulled the door open.

'Yes? Oh! Oh. *You.*'

He was leaning against the door-frame, casually, menacingly. Smiling, but there was a dark glitter in his eyes that made her take a step backwards.

Dimly she heard Fliss's voice drifting out from behind the closed door of the bathroom. 'Who is it?'

'It's OK,' she called back shakily, 'I've got it.'

He made no move, but raised an eyebrow. 'Am I disturbing anything?'

Yes! How about my sanity and my sense of self-respect for a start?

'No. What do you want?'

Oh, God. Did that sound how she thought it sounded? As if she might as well have said, Would you like to have sex with me? He shifted position slightly, straightening up, dipping his head, looking at her from under his long eyelashes in a way that made her feel the towel had just dissolved.

'Well. There are a number of answers to that question. The politest would be "dinner".'

'I can't. I told you. I'm going out. How did you find me?'

'I asked for your room number at Reception.'

Anna felt her heart plummet. Oh, help. She had a lot of explaining to do to Fliss. Or to him. Should she just come clean now?

But he had already turned and, slinging his jacket over one shoulder, started walking away along the corridor. Spinning back to face her, he shrugged and gave her a half-smile.

'Oh, well. It was worth one more try.'

Don't go! she wanted to shout, as the blood sang in her veins and her hormones cried out for her to follow him. He didn't turn back. She watched him disappear around the corner and then, shutting the door, slumped against it.

He was the man who was supposed to get everything he wanted, she thought despairingly—so why hadn't he persisted?

She let out a small cry of frustration. Because he hadn't wanted her enough.

Rounding the corner Angelo felt his hands harden into fists at his sides.

It seemed she had been telling the truth after all, and his instincts had been wrong. She was Felicity Hanson-Brooks, and she was staying in one of the most over-priced hotels on the Riviera, which was hardly the kind of accommodation one would associate with a committed eco-warrior.

He gave a small shrug. At least he'd found out now rather than taking any further trouble over her. Now he could forget all about her and get on with the deal.

'It's just as well we've been best friends since the dawn of time.' Fliss sighed enviously. 'If not I'd hate you. I knew it would look great on you—I just didn't realize *how* great.'

Distractedly Anna fingered the gossamer-fine oyster-coloured silk. She had submitted to Fliss's ministrations without a murmur, but all the time her head had been elsewhere. With Angelo. Wondering what would have happened if she'd said *yes*...

Forcing herself reluctantly back to reality, she managed a dazed smile. 'It's a fabulous dress. Thanks, Fliss. I'll just have to try very hard not to think about the millions of silkworms that died to make it.'

Fliss gave her a warning look. 'Good, because I'm sure that each and every one of them is up in heaven now agreeing that it was worth the sacrifice. Just look at yourself.'

Slowly Anna met her reflection in the full-length mirror. Gone was the smoky-eyed wild child. In her place stood a sophisticated society girl. The dress was short, a sort of baby doll style that managed to look demure while also being almost indecently sexy. The pearly silk fell in softly gathered folds from a yoke that reached just to the top of her breasts, and everything about her gleamed, from the tiny clusters of beads and crystals on the short bodice at the top of the dress to the little sequinned slip of a scarf Fliss had wound around her throat.

How could she look so smooth, so polished while underneath she was on fire?

She breathed out slowly, wondering how long the dizzying cocktail of hormones was going to keep pumping through her body.

Her hair, newly washed and straightened, hung in a dark silken curtain over her shoulders with no sign of the pink streaks beneath. She gave her head a little shake to reassure herself that they were still there, and flicked up the dress to see her denim hotpants underneath.

'You can't wear those, Anna! They'll spoil the line of the dress!'

'They're fine. I might go to the beach party later on, and I can hardly wear this there. The GreenPlanet guys wouldn't recognize me. *I* don't recognize me.'

'Excellent. That was the general idea.' Going over to the wardrobe, Fliss selected a shoe box from the stack on the floor. 'Try these.'

Inside was a pair of high-heeled sandals consisting simply of two slim diamanté bands. The room seemed to go very still for a moment as Anna looked down at them. When she lifted her head again her face was bleak.

'I can't wear them, Fliss. They're too high.'

'Ah. Then we have a problem. You know me and shoes—I don't do flat. You couldn't manage just for one evening?'

Anna shook her head. 'My ankle won't hold up in that position. The surgeon who operated was pretty clear about that. But thanks anyway.'

For a moment the two of them looked at each other in mute sadness, then Anna managed a watery smile.

'Oh, well, I'll just have to go barefoot. It's exactly the kind of stupid thing people expect me to do. You know how I hate to disappoint.'

They could hear the thud of the music long before they reached the party. As the lift plummeted downwards towards the basement nightclub the hot evening air vibrated with rhythm and with sensual promise, until the lift doors opened and the full impact of the party atmosphere was unleashed.

'Come on!' yelled Fliss, dragging her into the mass of sweating bodies. 'Let's dance!'

A problem with the bones in her ankle may have put paid to Anna's ballet career but it hadn't stopped her from dancing. The music was loud and pulsating, a wailing cacophony of guitar and drum that seeped into her spine and turned her bones to jelly. Smiling into Fliss's eyes, she tried to lose herself in the noise and movement.

But it was as if he were there with her. Every time she raked her hands into her hair and lifted it from her hot neck, in her head she was inviting the touch of his lips; every thrust of her hips in time to the throb of the music was wishful fantasy...

'Anna! *Anna!*'

She opened her eyes, dazed by yearning. Fliss stood in front of her, grinning. 'I need a drink!'

Anna stumbled after her through the crush, out into the relative quiet of the bar. Fliss came to an abrupt halt and cursed quietly. 'Uh-oh,' she said in a low voice. 'Quick. Turn round.'

Too late.

Coming towards them was a blonde in a tiny silver dress with waist-length platinum hair.

'Hi, Saskia!' said Fliss. 'You look great!'

Saskia inclined her head in silent agreement, but said, 'Oh, I feel dreadful. I haven't had a full night's sleep since we've been down here—too many parties. But you look marvellous, darling.' Kissing the air beside Fliss's left cheek, Saskia's eyes slid round to Anna and swept over her coldly. 'And what's this? Roberto Cavalli?'

'You were never the sharpest tool in the box, Saskia, but I'd have thought that even you could remember my name after five years in the same class at school,' Anna muttered.

'The dress. It's Roberto Cavalli.' Anna remembered that sly, insinuating tone so well. 'How kind of Fliss to lend it to you.'

Anna's chin shot up. 'How do you know it isn't mine?'

Saskia laughed. 'A Cavalli? Out of your league, Delafield. I hear that Ifford Park is having to throw itself open to parties of schoolchildren again this year. Sad, really.'

Noticing the storm clouds gathering in Anna's eyes, Fliss stepped in quickly.

'*Love* the hair, Saskia! It looks astonishingly real.'

Saskia looked smug. 'It *is* real. Swedish, apparently. Feel. *The Sunday Tribune* paid for it. I heard that they asked you to do that article too, Anna. Pity they didn't devote a bit more of the budget to you. But then—' she paused, flicking one long, sugary-pink acrylic nail '—I suppose you should think yourself pretty lucky you were asked to do it at all as it's an article about the *daughters* of the aristocracy. Trade Descriptions Act, and all that.'

The colour drained from Anna's face and beside her Fliss gave a shocked gasp.

'Anyway, must go. So many eligible bachelors to dance with, so little time. Enjoy the party, darlings.' She gave a little smirk as she teetered off and then turned back, her long hair swishing out like a pale vampire's cloak.

'Isn't it your birthday any day soon, Anna? I think I remember that it was pretty close to mine.'

'Yes.'

'Are you having a party this year? Do let me know if you are—I'd love to come.'

'Oh, she is *such* a cow. Anna! Wait!'

Fliss's voice reached Anna over the heads of the crowd as she pushed her way through but she didn't slow down. She knew it was stupid to let Saskia's barbed comments upset her, but as usual they had flown with unerring accuracy right to her rawest nerve.

She had been stupid to come.

Flinging herself through an unmarked door, she found herself in the merciful quiet of a dimly lit corridor. Heart hammering, she leaned back against the scarlet damask-covered wall and closed her eyes, waiting for the demons that snapped at her heels to retreat.

A moment later Fliss appeared, her face creased with concern.

'I'm sorry, Anna. I'd forgotten how poisonous she is. Or how jealous of you.'

'Jealous?' Anna gave a harsh laugh. 'I doubt it. She's mummy and daddy's little princess, rich and spoiled and pampered. What on earth has she got to be jealous of me for? I'm nothing. Nobody. As she likes to remind me whenever we meet.'

Gently Fliss took her arm. 'Don't. Come on. Let's go and get that drink. We may as well get tipsy at her expense.'

'No.' Anna pulled away. 'I'd rather drink cyanide. And I'm not going back in there either. Sorry, Fliss. I'm going to head back to the château—but I really should go and change out of this dress first.'

Fliss shook her head. 'It's fine. Keep it—it was pretty much made for you. Are you sure you'll be all right?'

'Absolutely.' Anna looked around for a way out. Several doors led off the dingy corridor and she made for the nearest one. 'Get back to the party and I'll call you soon.'

Without looking back, Anna pushed open the door and slipped through.

The room she found herself standing in was dark and smelled of cigar smoke and maleness spiked with excitement. And danger.

She'd found the casino.

Recklessly she strode forward, any hesitancy driven away by the adrenalin rush of fury and the persistent, painful drumbeat of desire in the cradle of her pelvis.

The beat of the music from the party was just discernible, but in here all was hushed. At the tables men in dinner jackets eyed each other through clouds of cigar smoke and spoke only when necessary. Standing behind them, women in evening dresses looked on, mentally spending the money their partners were winning or watching their plans evaporate in a disappointing hand, a luckless spin of the wheel. Their mask-like painted faces gave nothing away.

The tension in the air matched Anna's own pent-up feelings. Taking a glass of champagne from the tray held out by a waiter, she walked slowly past the roulette tables, trailing a hand along the backs of the velvet-upholstered chairs. She paused. A croupier was swiftly and impassively raking piles of chips off the emerald baize and Anna watched, fascinated, as the men seated around the table replaced them with more. The numbing warmth of the champagne started to steal down inside her, obliterating the pain of Saskia's venom.

'Any more bets?'

There was a further flurry of activity. In the halo of light cast by the Tiffany lamp hanging low over the table Anna could see beads of sweat breaking out on foreheads as men moved innocuous-looking piles of chips around.

How much money was represented on that table? she wondered idly. Enough to secure the future of the château?

She felt horribly restless.

The glass of champagne in her hand was deliciously cool against her feverish skin and she pressed it to her cheek, but it couldn't damp the fire that seemed to smoulder somewhere deep inside her. The back of her neck fizzed and tingled, each hair seeming to respond to some invisible stimulus, and she turned round.

He was standing a few feet away from her, the bright pool of light from one of the low-hanging lamps over the roulette table falling on his mane of dark blond hair and turning it into a halo of gold. One hand was thrust into his pocket, the other was loosely around the slender waist of an obscenely elegant blonde in a scarlet dress. Completely at ease, squinting through the smoke with narrowed eyes, he looked like a particularly wicked fallen angel—beautiful, but menacing. And utterly compelling. The expensively groomed, formally dressed men around him seemed like shadows, or bit players in the presence of his raw, charismatic sexuality.

She heard her own unsteady breath, felt the panicky race of her heart and the searing wild-fire heat of desire scorching through her veins.

And then he looked up.

Angelo drained his glass of champagne and forced himself to focus on the game.

It was one of those nights when he could do no wrong, and the chips on his side of the table were amassing at a rate that had the other men around the table sweating with fear. But he was bored.

When winning came too easily it was time to look elsewhere for excitement.

The man at the head of the table held up his hands in defeat and moved away as the croupier moved his depleted pile of chips away from him. His departure caused a little ripple of unease to go around the table, and the space he had left was not filled.

Angelo looked down at the table. Everyone else was playing cautiously now, and he idly considered walking away and leaving them while they still had something. But the black dog of his old despair was shadowing him and he knew he would keep going. Keep playing. Keep pushing himself to feel something.

Anything.

'Place your bets now, gentlemen, please.'

There was a rush of last-minute activity around the table as everyone placed their chips.

The blonde pouted and placed a perfectly manicured hand on one silk lapel. '*Chéri?* Rouge, I think this time, don't you?'

A smile lifted one corner of Angelo's mouth, but his narrowed eyes were as blank and expressionless as ever. He looked down, moving a towering pile of chips across the baize, pausing as he reached the solitary green marker. Considering.

Green.

The stack of coloured counters represented several hundreds of thousands of pounds, but around them his hands were perfectly steady. Green. It would be like making a bet with himself that he hadn't been wrong about her or who she really was. The odds might be outrageously, overwhelmingly against him, but there was a spark in the dark, dark, self-destructive heart of him that urged him onwards. The money was easily dispensable, easily replaceable...

It wasn't about the money.

It was about the danger. It was about that girl.

For a brief second Angelo closed his eyes and allowed himself to imagine the adrenalin rush of taking such a wild gamble—like a shot of alcohol on an empty stomach—astringent, invigorating, intoxicating. Even to lose would be something. Would make him feel *something*.

A sting.

Pleasure-pain.

Anything.

Opening his eyes again, he caught a flash of movement at the corner of his eye.

In the space left by the departed player, a shadow had fallen across the table. Cast by the light from the low lamps, it showed a woman's silhouette—the sweep of her shoulder, the curve and swell of a breast that, even though it was only two-dimensional shades of grey made him want to brush it with his fingers.

Her perfume was infinitely subtle, but he picked it up instinctively, like an animal on the scent of its prey. Or its mate. That scent of darkness vibrated like a low note inside his head, drowning out the shriller, sweeter, more sickly perfume of the blonde girl beside him.

Slowly he lifted his head.

Like heat-seeking missiles his eyes found hers, his gaze searing through the space that separated them. His expression remained absolutely still as his eyes travelled over her, taking in her perfect poise, the elegance of the pearlescent dress, the dark silken fall of her hair, stripping them away to try to find traces of the trembling, rebellious girl he knew lay beneath.

And then he noticed her bare brown feet.

Sensation struck him like a punch in the solar plexus. Sharp, breathtaking. Surprising.

A ripple of impatience went around the table and vaguely he was aware of the other players waiting. The croupier hesitated. *'Monsieur?'*

'No. I'm out. Settle my account, please.'

The croupier nodded respectfully and Angelo felt the blonde at his elbow wilt with disappointment. He didn't care.

He was fed up with playing, fed up with winning. He wanted the next challenge.

But when he looked up she was gone.

CHAPTER FOUR

ANNA didn't stop running until she had reached the bottom of the hotel steps and there was a taxi right in front of her. Heart hammering, she wrenched the door open and flung herself inside.

'Château Belle-Eden, *s'il vous plaît*. The beach. *La plage*.'

She saw the taxi driver glance at her curiously in his rear-view mirror, no doubt wondering why a girl in an expensive designer dress wanted to go to the beach at this time of night, but Anna didn't care. Anything to put some distance between her and Angelo Emiliani.

Green. He had been going to bet on green. To taunt her with the fact that he recognized her and knew exactly what she was up to. And to show her exactly how wealthy he was, and how little a loss like that would affect him.

She could still picture his hands as they moved the chips across the table. God, they were beautiful: slim, long-fingered, artistic, the skin smooth and golden in the light from the lamp above. Hands that could handle huge sums of money without a tremble—what else could they do?

A small sound escaped her—something between a whimper and a groan—as she stared wildly and unseeingly out of the window into the street-lit dark. It was completely new to her, this maelstrom of yearning that turned every nerve in her body into a taut string, vibrating with sexual awareness. She realized that she was shivering, sitting bolt upright on the back seat of the car, and with a conscious effort leaned back, looking up at the stars through the back window. But it was impossible to relax while every cell in her body was screaming in protest at being torn away from Angelo Emiliani.

'Stop the car! *Arret!*'

'*Mademoiselle?* Are you OK? We are almost there—at the beach. You want me to stop now?'

Up ahead Anna could see the turning off the main road on to the private track that led down to Belle-Eden's beach. In desperation and despair she rubbed her fingers over her stinging eyes.

'No. Sorry. Carry on. The beach will be fine, thank you.'

Pulling up at the top of the track, the driver looked worried. '*Ici, mademoiselle?* You will be all right on your own out here?'

'Fine, thank you. I'm home now.'

Stepping out into the warm night air, she breathed in the salt wind and heard the bass beat of music from the beach below. Hurriedly she paid the driver, suddenly desperate to get back to the uncomplicated company of her GreenPlanet friends and drink beer and dance.

Her bare feet sank into the sand as she ran to the edge of the dune, from where she could see the camp fire on the beach and the writhing bodies of people dancing to the music that came from some unseen source. Stumbling down towards them, she hitched the silk dress into the denim hotpants and put both hands up to her head, burying them in her hair, messing it out of the silken sleekness achieved by Fliss. The warm salt breeze caressed her bare skin. Every nerve-ending seemed to have heightened sensitivity and to be crying out for more.

'Anna! You're back! Cool dress…'

She moved through the crowd, closer to the camp fire. Normally there were only about twenty GreenPlanet campers, but tonight there were maybe double that number as friends had joined them. Gavin, one of the group's founders, broke away from the people he'd been talking to and came over, holding out a beer.

'OK?'

She nodded. 'I met him.'

Behind his small wire-framed glasses Gavin looked momentarily bewildered. 'Who?'

Anna almost wanted to laugh. How bizarre that Gavin shouldn't know who she was talking about when Angelo's face, his voice, his scent was filling her head and blurring the rest of the world behind a haze of longing.

'Angelo Emiliani.'

Even saying his name set fireworks off in her pelvis. She took a mouthful of warm beer and continued slightly breathlessly, 'I think you might be right about the pharmaceutical connection. I overheard him on the phone mentioning Grafton-Tarrant.'

Gavin nodded slowly, thoughtfully. 'Wow. Righteous. I'll get a couple of animal rights mates on to that in the morning. They might have heard something.' He had started to drift away towards some more people who had just arrived, but turned back and called over his shoulder, 'Nice one, Anna.'

She closed her eyes, inhaling deeply, feeling the rhythm begin to steal down inside her. It was more mellow than the vibrating wall of sound in the nightclub, but no less insistent for that. All around her people were swaying, together or alone, their eyes closed, their voices muted, totally relaxed.

With a thud of misery Anna knew she didn't fit in here either. She had told Fliss this was where she belonged, but looking around at the peaceful, carefree faces in the firelight she knew that wasn't true. Maybe it was all that talk of karma and chi, but these people had an inner peace, a deep-down conviction that Anna completely lacked. They had a passion for their cause.

She had passion. Passion that before now she had never imagined. The difference was that hers wasn't going to be satisfied by saving the nesting sites of a few woodpeckers.

Her throaty moan was lost beneath the music. Snaking her arms above her, she let her head fall backwards and circled her hips as all the pent-up tension of the last few hours seeped out of her and the music took over.

Anna knew plenty of people who had sought the solution to their problems in drink and drugs, and had seen the fallout that followed. The cure for the frantic beating of her heart and the tingling adrenalin that was surging through her veins was not to be found in the bottom of a bottle or the contents of a syringe, but in music.

When she was dancing she forgot everything. The past blurred into insignificance beside the rhythmic immediacy of *now*. It was the closest she ever came to being simply herself.

Above her the sky was vast and dark indigo, studded with stars. Underfoot the sand was soft and caressing, and around her the low murmur of conversation gradually faded as everyone lost themselves in the dancing.

No one noticed that they were being watched.

Angelo got out of his chauffeur-driven car and leaned against it, looking down over the beach.

A slight breath of wind caught his hair, lifting it off his forehead, and carrying to him the salt tang of the sea and, beneath it, the more earthy scent of woodsmoke from the fire.

There were more of them than he'd thought. But he could still pick out Felicity Hanson-Brooks without even having to try. It would have been much harder to ignore her presence, as his eyes seemed to be irresistibly drawn to her as she swayed and writhed to the hypnotic beat of the music.

So his instinct *had* been right and his private bet had been a winner. She was a spoiled little society princess who stayed in one of the best rooms at the Paradis and came down here to play at eco-warriors between social engagements. The smile that curved his lips in the darkness was one of triumph mixed with disdain.

Her money and status no doubt made her more of a dangerous adversary, but in many ways it made his position much simpler. So much easier to bring her to heel now he had lost all respect for her.

Swiftly he bent and unlaced his shoes, then took them off and tossed them into the back of the car. His socks followed, joining the dinner jacket and black silk tie he had discarded on the journey here, as he had followed the taxi.

'You want me to wait, sir?' The chauffeur's voice was entirely expressionless. 'Will you be going back to the hotel tonight?'

Angelo considered for a moment. 'No. Ask Paulo to prepare the yacht and send the tender down to the far end of the beach in—' he glanced at his watch, calculating '—half an hour.'

'The far end of the beach, sir?'

'Yes. Down there, where the forest slopes down to the water.'

'Very good, sir.'

Slamming the door, Angelo rolled up his exquisitely tailored trousers and set off at a run.

The music was loud, pulsing, good.

Anna scooped her hair up from her hot neck and held it loosely on the top of her head while the breeze cooled her skin. She was hot, she was tired, but she didn't want to stop dancing. As long as she kept moving she could deal with the torrent of emotions that raged within her. The torrent of desire.

It hadn't subsided. If anything, the music had intensified it, so that with every flick of her hips, every snaky undulation of her spine she could almost feel invisible hands upon her, holding her as she longed to be held. Every so often one of the boys would sway against her and the sheer nearness of another human being was like a spark on the dry tinder of her longing. But none of them even came close to providing what she needed.

She felt as if she were burning from the inside, and threw her head back to gasp for air. The music slowed, seguing seamlessly into Nina Simone, singing 'I Put a Spell on You'.

Anna shuddered with need and frustration and longing, sliding her hands through the tangle of her hair and arching backwards as two hands slid around her waist.

Strong hands, slipping down to her hips. She felt them writhe sinuously beneath their touch. Eyes closed, she leaned back against him as an image of Angelo Emiliani's beautiful hands swam into her head. Helplessly she found herself imagining that the hands that were now resting on the flat of her belly were his hands, that it was his strong thumb which was slowly caressing her quivering flesh.

A shot of pure molten desire shuddered through her.

With a low groan of anguish she wrenched herself away, but those hands pulled her back. Her eyes flew open and for a second she found herself staring into the narrow gleaming eyes that had haunted her all evening.

Her overwhelming feeling was of relief. He had found her. He had picked up the desperate signals her body had been sending out to his and responded. Thank God. Thank God. He was here. There was nothing more to do than give in to it. *This* was her passion. The white-heat generated by the friction between their bodies as they danced, his chest hard against her shoulders, his hands moving across her midriff, spanning her ribs, cupping her breasts—*that* was what she lived for.

She couldn't have said how long they danced like that, his body curved around hers in a way that was simultaneously passionate and protective and possessive. It was everything she wanted, but at the same time it wasn't enough. Her hands were raised above her head, knotted around his neck, her fingers exploring the hardness at its nape and the little dip at the base of his skull, then matting themselves into his hair. She loved the feel of him, but she needed more. She needed to see him.

To taste him.

With a smooth flick of her hips, she spun round so she was facing him, her eyes level with the hollow at the base of his throat. Her hands were still locked loosely around his neck and despite the pain in her ankle she found herself rising up on her tiptoes so that her pelvis was level with his. For long moments they swayed together like that—their hips meeting and grinding together in mutual hunger as the music wrapped itself around them in the darkness. Their eyes met, and held. It was like looking into a furnace.

His hands were on her waist now, their warmth and strength radiating through the thin fabric of the dress. His fingers slid downwards and for a second she registered the question in his eyes as they encountered the heavy denim top of her tiny shorts, low on her hips.

Slowly, without taking her eyes off his face, she crossed her arms and, taking hold of the hem of the dress, peeled it upwards over her head. Tossing it aside, she looked defiantly up at him.

Angelo let his gaze travel slowly over her.

Madre di dio, she was glorious, he thought grimly as his eyes swept downwards over the perfect breasts, barely concealed beneath a small white bikini top, and flat, narrow stomach, in the centre of which glittered a diamond piercing.

He felt liquid fire lick through his veins.

In a split second she was transformed from high-maintenance It-girl to rebellious grunge-chick but, *Gesù*, he liked it. Reaching out, he trailed a finger from the valley between her breasts down to her midriff, gently circling the silver stud above her navel.

His physical response to the feel of her skin was instantaneous. And uncomfortably strong.

The music gathered pace and intensity. He felt the shiver that vibrated through her at his touch and watched her face intently as she let her head fall back, her half-closed eyes proclaiming her desire.

It had started as a cynical ploy to find out what she was up to, but Angelo realised his actions were no longer motivated by business. Sliding his hands around to the small of her back, he pulled her towards him, bending his head to brush his lips across the exposed column of her throat.

This was pleasure. Pure, wicked pleasure, he thought, trailing the tip of his tongue slowly upwards to her jaw before their mouths met in ferocious mutual hunger.

And then suddenly his long fingers were in her hair, his hands cupping her head, so that the sound of the music and the sea were drowned out by the roaring of the blood in Anna's ears. Their bodies didn't touch, but she was aware of his height as he bent his head to hers, the strength and power that radiated from him like a physical force. Their open mouths devoured each other, desperately seeking, exploring, plundering until their teeth clashed and Anna tasted the iron-tang of blood.

Breathlessly she pulled away, then, catching sight of the expression of dark arousal on his perfect face, helplessly reached for him again. This time their bodies met too, as the music swept them up in its hypnotic beat. She was aware of her fingers digging into the hard muscles of his arms but was powerless to let go.

It was as if a dam had burst inside her and all the frustration, the anger, the loneliness and longing of the last ten years had come bursting out in a boiling tide of all-consuming lust. Like a volcano. She had always been too scared of intimacy, too frightened of rejection to give herself to a man, but suddenly all of those fears were simply swept away by the strength and simplicity of her need.

It didn't matter any more who she was. *This* was who she was.

The music had changed, become more upbeat, and people were drifting apart, going in search of another drink, as the spell of sensuality that had captured them all dissipated. But in their midst Anna and Angelo remained oblivious, until someone started clapping, drawing attention to them.

'Hey, Anna! Get a room!'

Dazed, she opened her eyes. Angelo's face was very close to hers, his eyes glittering in the firelight.

'*Anna?*' he murmured sardonically. 'I think we have some talking to do, don't you? Smile nicely at your friends, sweetheart, and let's walk.'

His fingers were like steel bands around her upper arm, but she was grateful. Without him holding her up, she wasn't sure she would have been able to stand. Behind them there were a few scattered whoops and catcalls as they stumbled away from the group in the firelight and felt the velvet darkness envelop them. The rhythmic swish of the sea grew louder as the music receded slightly and for a few moments they walked side by side in silence.

When he eventually spoke his voice was soft, but edged with menace.

'So, *Anna*, don't tell me—that was a staff party for the London office of Arundel-Ducasse. A team-building exercise?'

She tugged her arm free of his grip and took a couple of stumbling steps away from him, raising her chin as she spoke. 'I'm not an estate agent. I made that up. But I'm not ashamed of what I am.'

He stopped, slipping his hands into his pockets and looking down, as if looking at her was somehow distasteful.

'And what is that, *Anna*?'

'A member of GreenPlanet. Someone who's prepared to stand up for what they believe in and fight what they know is wrong.'

He sighed deeply and started walking again. 'Yawn, yawn, yawn. And what is so very wrong about me buying Château Belle-Eden, may I ask?'

The GreenPlanet group was far behind now and the sand beneath their feet was no longer soft and shifting but firm and damp, indicating that they were being inexorably drawn down towards the water's edge. Ahead of them she watched unseeingly as a small motor boat skimmed over the waves and came to a halt near the shore.

'Apart from the fact that you intend to cause environmental havoc by destroying most of the pinewoods for a landing strip?'

'You have done your homework.' He gave a small snort of cynical laughter. 'Don't worry—I'll arrange a decent relocation package for every displaced squirrel in the area.'

'Don't be flippant,' she snapped, then paused, watching his face intently in the darkness. This was a long shot, but she had nothing to lose. 'We don't like the sound of Grafton-Tarrant's involvement.'

That had him worried, she thought with a flash of triumph. He was suddenly very still, but in the silvery moonlight she could just make out a muscle flickering in the taut plane of his cheek.

'You interest me, Anna—?'

She hesitated for a fraction of a second. 'Field. Anna Field.'

'You obviously have a great passion for your cause.' His voice was like a caress in the warm night air. He took a step closer to her and caught hold of the ends of her slender sequinned scarf. 'But, *Anna Field*, I think it's only fair to warn you that I have a great deal of passion for this project. Which means that one of us will end up being hurt. And—' he lifted his hand and stroked the backs of his fingers down her cheek '—I think it's only fair to warn you that I don't *do* failure.'

Oh, I do, thought Anna savagely as a shudder of pleasure ricocheted through her at his touch. *Failure and I are old friends.*

She took a step backwards and was caught off balance for a second as her foot sank into the wet sand. At that moment a bigger wave rolled in, lapping over her feet and making her gasp at the sudden chill.

He caught her before she fell, scooping her up in his arms as if she were no heavier than a child. On the dark beach the intimacy of his nearness stole her breath away and banished every rational thought from her head. The cold water had spread goosebumps over her quivering flesh.

He radiated warmth.

And strength.

And sex.

His smile stopped her heart and stole her soul—and along with it her powers of resistance. 'I've got you now.'

'Put me—' She tried to struggle but knew the movement her body made was a desperate wriggle of invitation. His lips came down on to hers, silencing her and concentrating all her thoughts on the sensation of being in his arms, clasped against his chest, while he waded powerfully through the water.

She should feel scared. Angry. Indignant. But she didn't.

She felt cherished.

And so aroused she couldn't think straight.

Dazedly she opened her eyes as he stopped. The boat she had seen from further down the beach was right in front of them, and the man inside it stood as they approached.

'Wh—what the—? What are you—?'

'Shh.'

Effortlessly he lifted her in and vaulted over the side to take his place on the seat beside her.

'*Grazie*, Gianni.'

Anna looked around her with wild eyes as the speedboat engine started up with a roar. Her hair whipped her cheeks as it spun round and accelerated away, seeming to fly across the water away from the shore. 'What are you doing? Where are we going? I didn't ask—'

Gently he placed a long brown finger on her lips, then, as her words died away, trailed it down her throat and into the deep V between the triangles of her bikini. His eyes burned into hers.

'Not in so many words, *carissima*, but you can't deny that you want this as much as I do.'

'What?'

'Privacy. I don't doubt your friends are all very open-minded and liberal, but I prefer not to have an audience.'

She gasped in outrage. 'You're very sure of yourself, aren't you?'

He slid his hand beneath one of the triangles of fabric. Lazily he moved his palm downwards so that he was cupping her breast, and with exquisite, agonizing gentleness brushed his thumb across her hard nipple.

She couldn't restrain the cry that escaped her.

'Yes.' He smiled wickedly. 'With good reason, I'd say.'

With a barely there touch like the whisper of a butterfly's wings, his lips brushed hers, then he dipped his head and murmured against her neck, 'If you want to go back to the shore say so now. Gianni will turn round. But—' he nuzzled her earlobe '—I can assure you, you're quite safe. I'm a property developer, not a mass murderer.'

The blood was pounding in her ears, matching beat for beat the pulse that throbbed between her legs. Closing her eyes, she shook her head, trying to clear it, but instead arching her neck backwards and offering it to the caress of his mouth.

'I don't know who you are. I don't know anything about you…' she groaned.

'Exactly. That's what I intend to remedy. Give me the chance to show you that I'm not the complete philistine you imagine.'

This was madness. His hand rested lightly on her shoulder, in the sensitive curve at the base of her neck, sending cascades of shooting stars through her, so she couldn't concentrate on anything beyond the growing need inside her.

'*Tesoro?* Do you want to go back to the shore?' he whispered, his thumb tracing delicate circles beneath her ear.

'No.'

CHAPTER FIVE

'MAKE yourself at home. I need to go and have a quick word with the captain, if you'll excuse me.'

Stepping out of the tender on to the deck of a yacht, Anna glanced round at her sleek surroundings and tried desperately to look as if she were the sort of person who had been making herself at home on luxury super-yachts all her life.

'No problem. Where do I go?'

He gestured up a flight of steel steps. 'Why don't you go up to the top deck? I'll join you there in a moment.'

So this was Angelo Emiliani's natural habitat, she thought dazedly as she reached the top of the stairs and emerged into a breathtaking space. The deck stretched away from her in both directions—one end housing a seating area with huge white cushions and a steel-topped bar, while at the other a softly lit spa pool glowed azure-blue in the darkness.

She wandered over to the pool and sat on its tiled edge, trailing her fingers in the water. She'd expected it to be cool, but it was warm. Blood-warm. She withdrew her hand sharply and stood up again, scared of the sudden image she had of herself and Angelo in its silky embrace.

God, her senses were on such high alert she'd be getting turned on by her own shadow in a minute. It was as if her brain had been rewired, so that every thought brought her back on to the same tormenting loop of desire. She looked out across the dark stretch of water to the shore. On the beach the party continued, the bass thud of the music drifting across to her, the glow of the fire illuminating the pine forests on the cliff top and throwing the silhouettes of the dancers into dark relief.

They seemed a million miles away, like strangers rather than the people she lived with and had come to regard as a substitute family.

She'd got to know Gavin and the rest of the group when they had camped on the edge of the parkland at Ifford while they'd carried out a protest against a proposed motorway extension nearby. She had been at home recovering from the operation on her ankle at the time, facing a future without dancing. But it was the truth she had found out just before the operation—when the doctors had been investigating a possible genetic cause of the bone weakness from which she suffered—that had shattered her the most. That was why she had been ready to rebel against everything she had been brought up to stand for. Because all of it had been based on a shameful lie.

GreenPlanet had offered her an escape, a purpose and a very convenient way to get back at her father. But she could see now that it had never offered her anything deeper. At the time that had been enough.

Angelo stood at the top of the stairs, watching her for a moment. She was leaning on the deck rail, her face turned towards the bright point on the beach where the party was still in full swing. In the soft glow cast by the discreet lighting on deck he could see a wistfulness in her expression.

Taking a bottle of champagne from the chiller, he walked quietly towards her.

'Are you wishing you were still at the party?'

Startled, she spun round, a hand pressed to her chest as a small cry escaped her. 'I didn't hear you!'

He smiled, tearing the foil off the bottle. 'I know. You looked…' he paused, choosing the word carefully '…sad. I wondered if you were wishing you were back on the shore with your friends.'

She met his gaze steadily. 'No. I'm not. I'm glad I'm here.'

Her honesty surprised him. And excited him. He'd expected more of a show of resistance, though from the white-heat that had almost devoured them both back there on the beach he had known it would only be token. That was what most of the girls he knew would have done—made a great show of being uncertain or shy, and then stormed off in high drama when he wasn't interested enough to play along with persuading them.

'It was a good party,' he said gravely, easing the cork out of the bottle with his thumbs. Feeling the release of pressure as it came free and a plume of froth spilled over his hand. Coveting it.

'Yes.' It was little more than a harsh whisper.

He paused.

'Great dancing.'

He watched her close her eyes. Heard her drag in a ragged breath.

'Yes.'

Benedetto Gesù, this thing could easily spin out of control if he wasn't careful. His hand was perfectly steady as he poured the champagne into two slim flutes, but he was all too aware of the painful ache in his groin and cursed himself for it. Last night he'd had an actress in his bed whose blonde perfection had earned her the tabloid title 'cinematic icon' and had found himself struggling to go through the motions. So why, when faced with this rebellious stranger, was he suddenly like a walking advertisement for Viagra?

He handed the glass to her. For a moment neither of them spoke. She held his gaze bravely, though he could see that she was shaking violently.

'You're cold.'

Her chin lifted a fraction but her gaze didn't waver. 'No, I'm not cold.' She drew in a desperate breath.

I'm burning.

How could he stand there looking so bloody relaxed? she thought in anguish. What was it that Fliss had called him? *The Ice Prince.* It was a singularly appropriate name—obviously thought up by someone who had felt the polar chill of his detachment in the same way she was feeling it now. The passion that had threatened to engulf them both on the beach still raged within her, but he had obviously had second thoughts.

And then she felt him gently take the glass from her hand and put it down on a low table.

Her heart leapt and her stomach tightened.

'Bedtime, I think.'

His hand stroked down the length of her arm, sending an explosion of tiny sparks along her nerve-endings. Lacing his fingers though hers, he turned and she had no choice but to follow him, back down the steps up which she had come, down on to a lower deck with a huge dining table set out before a wide sliding glass screen. In the doorway he hesitated, looking down at her. The amusement and mockery that she had come to recognize in his blue eyes had gone, leaving in its place a brooding darkness that made her want to scream with longing.

'This way.'

His long brown fingers were still loosely entwined with hers and, looking hazily down at them, she allowed herself a dizzying moment of fantasy about the pleasure they were about to bring her. He stopped outside a polished wooden door in a discreetly lit corridor and held it open for her.

Walking over to the bed, she felt a lifetime of anticipation flutter like a cloud of butterflies in her stomach. This was what she had longed for. *This*, had she but known it at the time, was the logical conclusion of all those girlhood wedding fantasies.

She sat primly on the edge of the huge bed—or as primly as she could, given that she was wearing only the briefest bikini top, behind which her nipples were all too clearly visible—and forced herself to look up at Angelo. It was a little like looking into the sun.

He was dazzling.

Tall, broad, effortlessly and stomach-meltingly gorgeous, he stood in front of her, towering over her. But his face was emotionless. With a thrill of dark excitement she wondered if he was going to ask her to strip.

'You should have everything you need. The bathroom is through there. Just pick up the phone if you need anything and one of the crew will bring it to you.'

Anna felt as if the world were tilting beneath her as the full horror of his words hit her. A whimper of shame and panic rose in her throat and she concentrated every ounce of self-control she possessed on swallowing it.

How could I have got it so wrong? How could I have made such a pitiful fool of myself?

It was pride that enabled her to raise her head and look him in the eye. Muster a small brittle smile. Say a polite, hollow thank you.

But when the door finally shut behind him she threw herself on to the bed and, seizing a pillow, howled out her fury and humiliation into the muffling layers of finest Siberian goose down.

Walking away wasn't easy, but returning to the upper deck, Angelo grimly congratulated himself.

Whatever he had felt on the beach, she *was* business, not pleasure.

He wasn't a man who was overly troubled by conscience. Life had not showered a steady stream of blessings upon him, so he worked on the principle that if he wanted something he had to get it himself. That had made him ruthless.

Reckless.

With money. With rules. With people.

And tonight he had wanted her, but something had stopped him. Some sort of hitherto undiscovered sense of chivalry, which had prevented him from taking her just because he could.

Sometimes he wondered if the nuns in the orphanage still prayed for his immortal soul. Maybe, finally, their prayers were being heard. Maybe there was a glimmer of hope that he wouldn't be consigned to eternal damnation after all.

He gave a short bitter laugh.

Or maybe he just wanted to make her wait. Who knew how long it might take to get the sale of the château completed? It wouldn't do to rush things. The longer he kept her on a slow-burn, the better.

And the more satisfying.

In Anna's dream she was a child again, sitting on her mother's knee and being rocked.

She looked up into her mother's eyes, those blue-green eyes she remembered so well, and then a really odd thing happened. They were her mother's eyes, but they were also Angelo Emiliani's eyes, and something about that bothered her. She felt safe, protected, loved, but unaccountably uneasy.

When she woke up the rocking continued. For a moment she lay there, as fragments of the events of yesterday and last night came back to her. She sat up with a start.

The boat was moving.

Throwing herself out of bed, she stood up and looked wildly around her. The view through the window showed nothing but sea and sky. She made a sharp exhalation of fury and had reached the door of the cabin before she stopped.

She was still stark naked.

She was in the middle of the ocean and the only items of clothing she had with her were a bikini and a pair of hotpants.

Oh, and a sequinned evening scarf—which would no doubt make all the difference should formal dress be required. Collapsing back on to the bed, she pulled the covers up over her head and let out a howl of rage and frustration.

'Ah, so you're awake.'

In the darkness beneath the covers she felt her eyes widen in horror and for a second she froze, hoping she'd imagined that dry, mocking voice. But then the covers were drawn back and she found herself staring up into those wicked eyes.

In the clear light of morning his beauty came as a fresh shock. Naked to the waist and wearing only a pair of long shorts, his blond hair was tousled and untidy. He looked more like a carefree golden surfer-boy than a billionaire businessman.

Which was horribly unfair.

Snatching the covers up to cover her breasts, she sat up and glared at him. 'What the hell is going on?'

That cool, unruffled smile. 'I brought you coffee.'

'I don't want coffee!'

'I believe the polite response is "thank you very much". I can assure you, you're very privileged. I don't usually do this sort of thing, but I looked in on you earlier and you were rather… exposed. My crew can cope with most things, but a naked eco-warrior might just prove too much, even for them.'

It almost had for him. Lying on top of the cream sheets with her pink hair tumbling over her face and the diamond stud in her navel rising and falling with every sleepy breath, she had looked wild but unbelievably sweet. Like a panther cub. He had to keep reminding himself that if he wasn't careful she could do real damage.

Anna took a deep steadying breath and pulled the sheet more tightly around her. Making a huge effort to keep her voice level, she looked up at him.

'Look, Angelo… Last night was…' *Oh, God, don't blush. Don't behave like a pathetic, inexperienced kid. Don't give it away.* 'A huge mistake. I shouldn't have come here.'

'So why did you?'

He had set the coffee down on the bedside table and was looking at the newspaper he'd had tucked beneath his arm. He looked totally absorbed, as if what she was saying was a minor distraction.

'I didn't have much choice,' she hissed, thoroughly nettled by his obvious unconcern.

He looked up at her with a slight puzzled inclination of his eyebrows. It was almost as though he'd forgotten she was there for a second. 'Sorry? That wasn't how I remember it. I think I asked you if you wanted to go back to your "friends" on the beach—' he looked back down at the newspaper with a faint smile '—and you said no.'

'I didn't know then that a cruise around the Med was on the itinerary.'

'I see. A quick screw. That's all you had in mind, was it?' He glanced back up at her. 'I'm hurt.'

He didn't look hurt. He look supremely unconcerned, hugely pleased with himself. And immensely bloody gorgeous.

Anna gritted her teeth. 'We didn't have sex.'

'No. But you wanted to.'

Oh, God, the bastard.

Tugging the sheet, she wound it around herself and got up. Sitting in bed she felt at far too much of a disadvantage to be having this conversation. Standing up, she raked a hand through her hair and made a huge effort to keep the hysteria out of her voice.

'Look, I didn't have anything in mind. I wasn't exactly thinking straight. I don't know—maybe I drank more than I thought. I was upset and—'

'Upset about what?'

She shook her head. 'Doesn't matter,' she said hastily. 'What matters now is that I have to get back. I have stuff that I need to do.'

Rubbing a hand through his already dishevelled hair, he strode towards the door. Anna squeezed her eyes shut as he passed within a few feet of her, unable to trust herself not to reach out and touch the body that had haunted her dreams all night. At the door he paused and looked at her with great seriousness.

'How good are you at swimming?'

'Very good.'

He nodded gravely. 'It's probably about ten kilometres back to shore. Just as well you brought your bikini.'

Anna gave a howl of rage, picked up a book and hurled it in the direction of his head. It missed and she reached for another, but he was too quick for her. The next thing she knew, he was beside her and had caught her wrist in a steely grip.

'Enough.'

She let herself relax completely for a moment, until she felt his fingers slacken slightly, then seized her chance and gave an almighty lunge to break free.

'*Not* enough. Not nearly enough.'

Her only thought was to put as much distance between them as possible, but the bed was in the way. Clasping the sheet to her, she leapt on to it and stood, legs apart, chest heaving, looking down at him.

He raised an eyebrow. 'Well, now you come to mention it…'

In one swift movement he had reached out and swept her legs from beneath her so that she tumbled down on to the soft cushion of pillows. High on adrenalin, she struggled upright, but he was already on top of her, pinning her arms above her head with one strong hand as easily as if she had been a child. Above her, only inches away from her face, his chest curved. If she lifted her head she could probably brush his nipple with her lips. Her breath was coming in huge, shaky gasps, but the rise and fall of his chest was as steady as ever.

Frantically she thrashed beneath him, desperately trying to ignore the treacherous, tell-tale stickiness at the top of her thighs, praying he wouldn't notice that she was virtually at the point of orgasm.

Their eyes met and locked. Neither of them spoke and the only sound was the ragged gasp of Anna's breathing.

His eyes glittered down into hers, narrow and knowing. Slowly, lazily he reached out with his free hand and trailed a leisurely finger along her collar-bone. She was no longer holding the sheet—all it would take would be one flick of his wrist and she'd be naked and exposed to his glittering gaze.

'If you were hoping to persuade me to take you back to shore, this is hardly the best way to go about it.'

Her eyes flashed fire and fury at him.

'Why? Would you prefer it if I *begged*?' she spat.

He laughed huskily and released her wrists. '*Amore mio*, that would be equally alluring, and therefore equally counter-productive.'

She rolled out from beneath him, not trusting herself to spend one more second in such close proximity with his long golden body. 'I'm not hoping to *persuade* you of anything. I'm demanding that you take me back. Today.'

'Or else?'

'Or else I'll call the police.'

'You have your mobile?'

'You know I haven't'

She had nothing, and he knew it. Not a change of clothes, not a toothbrush, and certainly not a mobile. Furiously she swung her legs out of the bed and stood up, yanking the sheet from under him and wrapping it around herself again.

He sighed and stood up.

'So I guess you'll be wanting me to lend you my satellite phone, which is a bit much considering you intend to use it to have me arrested for…well, what? Kidnapping you? Forcing myself upon you against your will?'

She blushed. 'No.'

If only.

Unhurriedly he ran a hand through his hair, making it stand up in spiky golden tufts that only served to accentuate his perfect bone structure. Turning towards the door, he said, 'In that case, may I just suggest you come along for the ride? You never know, you might learn something.'

She tossed her head and threw him a disdainful look. 'What could I possibly learn from you?'

He paused and half turned back, studying her silently for a moment with his head tilted to one side.

'We're heading for a property I finished work on last year. It's been bought by a certain celebrity with a bit of an environmental conscience and developed to be as environmentally friendly as possible. I'd like to show it to you. Maybe you'll learn not to believe everything that's been written about me. Maybe you'll find I'm not the devil incarnate after all.'

'I doubt it,' she spat. But he had already gone and she was speaking to a closed door.

CHAPTER SIX

Two hours later Anna had to admit that, whatever Angelo Emiliani was, life aboard his yacht wasn't at all bad. She had idled away some time in the spa pool, until the steward, Paulo, had brought her a delicious brunch of fresh fruit and warm, sweet brioche and coffee, and now she was lounging on the soft white cushions feeling heavy and replete.

There was something very liberating about being out in the middle of the ocean. Something therapeutic about literally sailing away from your problems. Last night, and Saskia's malice, seemed light years ago. Here there was no need to apologise for who she was.

Who she wasn't.

She had spent her early life feeling torn between England and France—Ifford Park and Château Belle-Eden—but, closing her eyes and letting her head fall back against the cushioned lounger, she realised she'd missed the obvious solution. Somewhere in between.

'Anna.'

Her eyes opened slowly and she stretched luxuriously. 'Hmm?'

'I don't know what you do for a real job, but you certainly could sleep on a professional basis. It's time to wake up. We're here.'

Anna stumbled to her feet quickly. Too quickly. There was a roaring in her ears and she almost lost her balance.

Angelo's hand shot out to steady her and when the fog cleared from behind her eyes she found herself staring at the bronzed plane of his chest. She shook him off and took a step backwards.

'I don't usually sleep like that. I don't know what came over me. Maybe it's the sea air.'

He was looking at her with unconcealed amusement. 'It certainly can't be the exercise—although not for want of trying.'

Why could he make her blush so easily?

His gaze swept down over her, taking in the skimpy bikini top and minute denim hotpants. 'Before we go ashore, would you like to get changed into something a little more...discreet?'

'Oh, yes. Silly me. I'll just go and choose something from the selection of cruisewear I packed in preparation for this trip, shall I?'

'I'm sure I can find something that would fit.'

'Why, Angelo, how fascinating. Do you have a large selection of ladies' clothes in your wardrobe?'

'No, but I have a number of visitors to the yacht who've left things.'

'Oh, puh-leese. If you think I'm going to wear something belonging to one of your harem of mistresses, you can think again.'

'I don't know why you find the thought so unpleasant, *tesoro*. I recall that last night you were pretty keen to join them. Anyway, if you're going to be stubborn...'

She looked at him for a moment, speechless with humiliation and loathing.

'Let's just go, shall we?'

Arriving at the private landing stage of Villa Santa Domitilla, Angelo held out his hand to help Anna from the tender. She ignored it.

'Where are we?'

Angelo was already halfway along the boarded walkway and spoke over his shoulder. 'Let's just say it's one of Italy's undiscovered islands. The celebrity who's bought this property would be extremely unhappy about having its location given away. Especially to known troublemakers.'

'I thought you said it was very environmentally friendly?'

He nodded.

'Well, in that case, they have nothing to fear from us. It's only projects that put personal profit before responsibility to the planet that we campaign against.'

Why do I bother? He's not even listening, she thought furiously as she trailed after him up a set of steep steps cut into the rock. Despite the fact that it was scorching hot, Anna was annoyed to see how cool Angelo looked in a pair of long cotton surf shorts and a white linen shirt.

Why hadn't she taken up his offer of borrowing something to wear? Despite her olive skin, she could already feel the sun burning on to her shoulders and she felt uncomfortably exposed in the tiny bikini top and hotpants.

Exposed and—when she saw the magnificent honey-coloured house in front of them—entirely underdressed.

'It used to be an old convent,' Angelo explained, keying a number into the security pad beside the huge wrought iron gates. 'The thickness of the stone walls made it ideal from an energy-saving point of view.' The gates swung open and he sauntered through, while she hung back.

'What's the matter? I thought you'd be desperate to see all your principles in practice.'

Folding her arms, Anna looked up at the building. 'I'm not going in.'

'I see. Why not?'

'I don't need the whole marketing and PR package, Angelo. I'm sure you're very good at talking the talk. It won't change anything.'

He'd stopped and now began to stroll slowly back towards her. His long limbs moved like liquid. Pure animal grace.

She swallowed.

He shrugged. 'So, just enjoy the trip. Soon enough it'll get out who's bought this place and you'll be able to tell all your friends that you've been here.' He carried on walking up the narrow path to the front of the villa.

She stamped her foot and followed him up the path. 'I wouldn't stoop to celebrity *name-dropping*,' she said scornfully. 'I couldn't care less who this house belongs to, it doesn't alter the fact that what you're planning to do at Château Belle-Eden is wrong!'

Smiling to himself, Angelo resisted the temptation to turn round and look at her.

Perhaps it wasn't fair to tease her, but he couldn't help it. She was so quick to rise to the bait and so funny when she was angry. And she was such a bloody cliché, with her tired old environmental platitudes.

He frowned.

A cliché, but a mystery too. He still wasn't entirely sure who she was. His PA in London was right now trying to find information on Anna Field, but when he'd spoken to her just before setting out had come up with nothing. It was possible that she was a runaway, of no fixed address, which would explain why she had fallen in with those appalling campaigners. They probably had some sort of group squat.

The thought horrified him.

Reaching the front door of the villa, he stopped and waited for her. She was a little way behind him and he watched her trail slowly up the path, between the artfully planted 'wildflower' borders which his celebrity client had commissioned at a cost of thousands from Italy's top garden designer. The shadows played across her glistening amber-coloured skin, the sunlight glinting off the diamond in her navel. A bumblebee, heavy and clumsy with pollen, blundered through the flowers and came to land on her arm. She stopped, her tongue darting out between moist pink lips as, with an expression of rapt concentration, she carefully scooped it into her hand and placed it on a leaf. It was the first time he'd seen her give in to the softness he sensed beneath that rebellious veneer, and he felt an unexpected twist in his gut.

Anna looked up at the building in front of her. It was solid and square, a cloistered walkway running the length of the ground floor and providing a sheltered position for olive and citrus trees in huge terracotta pots. The golden stone was mellow with age, and the overall impression was of timeless peace and spirituality.

The front door was open, Angelo having gone in ahead of her. She walked into the centre of the hallway and turned slowly around, taking in the acres of polished wooden floor and the galleried landing above, from which were suspended vast modern canvases depicting images that reminded Anna of photographs in her biology textbook at school.

'It's…' She hesitated, gazing up at the massive twisted metal chandelier that hung above them, which on closer inspection seemed to be constructed from used car parts. The contrast of the stark interior with the gracious exterior of the building was like a slap in the face.

'It's utterly *hideous*.'

She'd intended to hurt him, she realized, but she was completely unsuccessful. He smiled and, with his hands in his pockets, walked casually across the hallway. 'I'm inclined to agree. However, that's not the point.'

'Not the point? How can you say that? This was a convent—an ancient place of worship and contemplation and devoutness—and you've made it look like some soulless New York loft apartment. It's totally disgusting!'

He'd reached one of the doorways that opened off the hall and paused, leaning nonchalantly against it. 'There you go again.'

'What?'

'Making assumptions.' His voice was very quiet. 'Firstly, *I* didn't make it look like anything. My brief stopped with the building itself. The interior was entirely the work of the client and her team of lifestyle gurus, interior designers, feng shui experts and spiritual analysts. Secondly, you're assuming I don't agree with you. And, thirdly, don't ever make the mistake of thinking that convents are all places of *devoutness*.'

There was a savagery in his tone that made her look at him sharply. But his face gave nothing away. 'I thought you'd be thrilled that the floor is reclaimed hardwood, that all the artwork was commissioned from a local women's co-operative and shows magnified images of the plant-life on the estate, and the chandelier was made out of recycled industrial parts.' He smiled sardonically. 'Come up and I'll show you the rest.'

He was almost at the top of the stairs now and she had to choose between following him or remaining alone in the hallway. Mutinously she stared up at him, her arms crossed.

'No, thanks. I think I've seen enough.'

'Suit yourself. But, if you'll excuse me, I've got a couple of things to attend to. I may be a while, so make yourself comfortable.'

'I think that's pretty unlikely in this—' she said contemptuously, but was interrupted by the ringing of his mobile phone.

He answered impassively, striding away from her along the corridor, out of earshot. Left alone, Anna shivered, hugging her arms around her all too exposed flesh.

She was just about to leave the house and wait for him outside when, with a flash of defiant insight, she realised that by doing so she would be playing right into his hands. The call was obviously one he didn't want her to overhear, and was maybe information about the château or something to do with Grafton-Tarrant.

She was wasting a golden opportunity with her immaturity

and her pathetic inability to rise above his physical attributes. It was stupid and embarrassing. He was beautiful, but he was also the person who was about to rob her of the only place that tied her to a happier past.

Swiftly she made for the stairs and took them two at a time. Up on the galleried landing she paused, listening intently, but there was no sound. The silence played on her senses, making her both nervous and full of anticipation as she strained to hear the deep rumble of his voice.

All she could hear was her own heartbeat.

Fast.

Excited.

Rows of closed doors stretched away from her. Tentatively approaching one, she pressed her ear to the wood—reclaimed, no doubt—not that she could have cared less—and listened.

Nothing.

She slid along to the next door and listened again.

Silence.

In frustration she opened the door and looked inside. It was a bedroom, dominated by the biggest bed she'd ever seen. Sulkily she wandered in, her bare feet practically disappearing into the thick white carpet. It was decorated in the same aggressively modernist style, the huge canvases on the walls depicting unintelligible blobs and shapes which looked vaguely erotic. Anna stopped in front of one that seemed to show the curve of a woman's breast against the sweep of a male buttock.

Or was she imagining that?

She tried to imagine it hanging in the château, and felt a shiver of distaste ripple down her spine.

Of course it was distaste.

She tore her gaze away abruptly and pushed open the door into an *en suite* bathroom. Or shower room, she mentally amended, looking round the spartan cell derisively. There was nothing so luxurious and water-wasteful as a bath tub in there.

In fact, maybe it wasn't finished, she thought, taking a step forward. The room was lined in tiny glowing green glass tiles like the scales on a mermaid's tail, but apart from that it was empty.

Suddenly jets of water exploded on to her bare skin from all sides, soaking her. She screamed and tried to dart out of the way, but the whole room was filled with tiny water outlets and she had moved directly into the firing line for freezing cold jets.

She screamed again. Louder.

Just as suddenly and unexpectedly as it had begun, the water stopped. Dripping, shivering, incoherent with shock and fury, she pushed back her streaming hair from her face and looked up to find Angelo lounging in the doorway.

Laughing.

CHAPTER SEVEN

'I SEE you discovered the wet room.'

Anna tried to frame a coherent sentence but found herself able to do nothing more than mouth impotently. The only words that came to mind were too offensive for her to even utter.

'Pretty impressive, no? Designed to use as little water as possible. All the shower jets incorporate tiny vacuum pumps to aerate the water as it comes out and so increase the pressure.' He'd been lounging against the door-frame, but now he levered himself upright. 'That way, you get a very powerful shower while using a minimum amount of water, and the whole thing is operated by sensors.'

'Thank you,' she spat. 'I think I'd just about worked that bit out for myself.'

The second part of the sentence came out as a dry croak as she watched him unbuttoning his shirt. She took a step backwards, unable to take her eyes off the rippling golden chest that was gradually being revealed.

'What are you doing?'

He looked up and grinned as he slipped his shirt off. For a fleeting moment she thought she might pass out.

He held out the shirt to her.

'Here. Put this on.'

'No, thanks. I'm fine.'

She made to walk past him, but as she did so he caught hold of the tie at the back of her sodden bikini. And pulled.

She breathed in sharply, making a small shivering sound.

In an instant he was behind her and, with swift, capable hands, had drawn the tiny triangles of fabric over her head, in the same seamless movement wrapping his shirt around her. She was aware of nothing but the warm scent of him, imprinted into the whisper-soft linen, the firm pressure of his hands.

'Now, take off those wet shorts.'

She spun round to face him. 'No! No—I—'

He took a single step towards her and reached out. She had to bite her lip against the gasp that sprang from her, the flicker of fiery arousal that licked up her belly in anticipation of his touch. But he only took hold of the shirt and started to do up the buttons. Through a mist of agonizing desire, she glanced up at his face.

His eyes gave nothing away.

He had moved upwards and was now buttoning the shirt over her bare breasts. She was aware of the painful thrust of her nipples against the fabric and closed her eyes for a second in blissful submission.

'There. Perfectly respectable. It almost comes down to your knees, so you're perfectly safe to take off your shorts. I won't look.'

Her eyes fluttered open and she swung blindly away from him, fumbling with the stiff button of the wet denim. But her hands were slow and clumsy with confusion. 'I—can't.'

'Then allow me.'

Gently he drew her towards him. Unable to raise her eyes to meet his, she watched, mesmerized, as his long elegant fingers undid the button of her shorts, aware of the flat plane of his tanned stomach only inches from her own. His thumb brushed the quivering flesh of her midriff, sending a cascade of shooting stars up her spine, almost making her knees give way beneath her.

Slowly, he tugged down the short zip and, slowly, deliberately slid the wet denim downwards. Helplessly she felt her hips wriggle beneath his hands, as if they had a mind of their own and were desperate to free themselves of the layers that separated her from him.

He dropped to his knees in front of her and she let her head fall backwards, lifting her hands and instinctively winding them into her wet hair as she fought to keep control of the murmurs of pleasure his touch aroused in her. His warm hand slid down one leg, then the other, stopping at her foot, his fingers tracing a swift arc of fire across her instep before gently picking it up and making her step out of the shorts. Looking down, she saw him bent before her, his tousled dark blond hair contrasting with the paler gold of the skin of his bare shoulders, beneath which the muscles flexed and rippled. Dimly she was aware of her own fingers twisting her hair into knots of desire, and she opened her eyes as he straightened up before her.

His thumb kneaded her parted lips, his fingertips caressing the hollow beneath her jaw, then trailing down the long, exposed column of her throat as she arched her back and pressed her hips to him.

She ached.

His fingers crept into the damp tangle of her hair, supporting the heavy weight of her head as she waited for his lips to meet hers. He brought his head down to brush his mouth against the side of her neck, where the pulse beat frenziedly beneath her damp skin.

'Time to go,' he murmured dryly. 'A-list celebrities can be very touchy about complete strangers having sex in their bedrooms.'

Her eyes flew open as he drew away and bent to scoop her discarded shorts up off the floor. Without looking back, he walked perfectly steadily across the room to the door.

Anna dragged a hand across her burning lips and swore softly.

Striding after him, she caught up with him in the doorway and snatched her clothes from him. Then she ran ahead of him down the stairs and out into the sunlight.

Closing the front door behind him, Angelo paused briefly and rubbed the frown from his forehead.

Careful, he warned himself, but his knuckles were white on the large iron door handle. He needed to get this deal completed and return Anna to the safety of dry land, because if this carried on much longer he knew his resolve wouldn't hold and he'd have to bed her.

He wanted to, but he'd glimpsed a vulnerability in her that scared him. It was that moment when he'd done the buttons up on the shirt. It had made him think of Lucia.

He shook his head and gave the door a last little push to check that it was closed properly and turned to go down the steps. He could see her walking ahead of him down the path back to the gate that led to the jetty, the tails of his shirt reaching just above her knees. She was sexy as hell, he thought, and she had walked into this situation with her eyes wide open—she must be pretty sure of herself to have done that. As he watched, she dragged a hand through her hair, making the pink streaks flash in the sun. A sardonic smile spread across his face.

She was nothing like that other little girl he had let down all those years ago in the orphanage. Lucia had been a child—a vulnerable child—who had relied on him as her only source of support in a harsh, loveless world, and he would never forgive himself for what had happened to her. But this was different. Anna was strong and spiky and rebellious—she could look after herself. He was just imagining the trembling little girl beneath the surface.

His expression was stony as he set off down the path after her.

He'd ring his PA as soon as they were back on the yacht and see if she'd had any word from Ifford's people about what the hell was going on at their end. The sooner those papers were signed the better. For his sanity.

Storming back into her cabin, Anna slammed the door behind her and threw herself on to the bed.

She wanted to scream, she wanted to tear things up, she wanted to smash Angelo Emiliani's perfect face to a pulp.

But mostly, she admitted to herself with a low moan, she wanted to have sex with him. Wild, uninhibited, magical, mind-altering sex.

For about twenty-four hours.

She rolled over and buried her face in her arms. The situation was unbearable. She was in the middle of nowhere with the most beautiful man she could imagine and he was playing some kind of sadistic game with her. She remembered her conversation with Fliss—how she'd said that he had a reputation for being icy cool. She hated men like that—the kind who messed with your head—and, Lord knew, there were plenty of them around. Always the best-looking ones, of course, the ones who would pursue you and flatter and flirt until you succumbed and slept with them, and then you wouldn't see them for dust. Until you spotted them again across a crowded bar, doing exactly the same with someone else.

Roseanna Delafield wasn't going to be a notch on anyone's bedpost.

She'd kept herself well clear of all that; packed her heart on ice and buried her desires beneath a thick layer of cynicism and denial. But here she was, stranded at sea with nowhere to run. Nowhere to hide from the feelings he'd unleashed in her.

Bastard.

She sat up, suddenly blindingly, furiously angry. How dared he put her through this, with no concern whatsoever for her feelings? No—worse than that. He wasn't unconcerned about her feelings—he was actively *enjoying* watching her squirm.

Roughly she shrugged off his shirt and slipped back into her bikini. So what if it was still damp? At least it didn't carry his scent on it, tantalizing her.

Restlessly she paced the length of her small cabin, her mind racing, trying to think up a plan to get away from him. With no contact with the outside world, she could hardly claim a sudden death in the family or some similar crisis. Besides, she doubted whether Angelo Emiliani would be human enough to let a little thing like that change his plans. Business, maybe, but a personal matter…

She stopped dead.

That was it.

She groaned out loud, cursing her own stupidity. Of course—why hadn't she realized? He hadn't brought her here to try to change her mind. He'd brought her to keep her out of the way until the sale had gone through. What he didn't know was that that wasn't going to happen without her going to Nice to sign the papers.

That changed everything. She was in no hurry to leave now. Suddenly, unexpectedly, she found she was holding all the aces and the game had started to get a lot more interesting.

At seven o'clock precisely there was a knock at her door. Despising the treacherous leap of excitement in the pit of her stomach, Anna yanked it open.

It was Paulo, the steward.

'Dinner is served in the saloon, *signorina*.'

'Oh. Thank you, Paulo, but I'm not dressed. I don't have anything else to wear…'

'It would be no trouble to find something, if you would be more comfortable, *signorina*?'

'No,' she said curtly, 'I don't mind, but I thought that maybe Signor Emiliani might object.'

Walking down the corridor in the direction of the saloon,

Paulo turned and grinned. 'I don't think so, *signorina*. Here on *Lucia* we have a pretty laid-back dress code, and the evening is still beautifully warm.'

The sliding doors of the saloon were open and soft orchestral music was pouring out of the sound system into the warm air. Anna could see the table beyond, softly lit against the pastel-hued evening. It was beautiful, but as she approached her heart sank.

'There's only one place set, Paulo… Is Signor Emiliani not dining?'

Paulo didn't quite meet her eye. 'I'm sorry, Signorina Field, but he has a lot of work to do. He's very busy taking calls right now, but he might be able to join you later. In the meantime, please take a seat. Would you like some champagne or is there anything else I can get you? A cocktail?'

'Champagne is fine, thank you.'

It was irritation that was hardening like cement in her chest, she thought grimly. Not disappointment. Not hurt. She was annoyed by his rudeness, that was all. Yet again he had managed to make her feel about two feet tall, and about as sophisticated as a school kid. There was no way she was sitting down at that ridiculously big table to eat on her own, she thought mutinously, wandering over to the deck rail and looking out over the darkening ocean as uniformed crew brought out numerous dishes and plates arranged with food.

She wasn't hungry. Or not in a way that could be satisfied by eating.

The evening was a cliché of romantic perfection—the flaming sun just dipping down into the sea, spreading shimmering trails of rose pink across the glassy surface, but its beauty only intensified the yearning inside her. Finishing the glass of champagne, she trailed restlessly back into the saloon, where a nineteen-fifties style jukebox stood against the wall.

She surveyed the selection with a measure of disdain, which

quickly turned to grudging respect. Angelo Emiliani had better taste than the average billionaire property tycoon, she thought sourly. Or maybe when you were as rich as he was you had 'people' to choose your music for you? She programmed in a few songs she liked, upped the volume and drifted back outside again.

The table stood under a sort of canopy created by the mezzanine floor of the deck above which projected outwards, supported by slim chrome pillars. Passing it, she pulled off an artichoke leaf and trailed it in warm hollandaise before lasciviously sucking it.

Oh, God. Why did everything have to bring her back to the same agonizing place?

The lights from the saloon spilled out over the deck, casting long shadows in the hazy evening. The sun had disappeared now and the stars were beginning to come out in little glittering groups, like celebrities at happy hour, but there was nothing else to see. She felt all alone—a beacon of burning desire adrift on a darkling ocean.

There was a whirr and click from the jukebox as one track ended and another one began. She moaned softly as she recognized it. Nina Simone—'I Put a Spell on You'.

The music was like a match to a petrol-soaked rag and the longing she had been trying to extinguish inside her burst instantly into flame. Slowly, languorously she reached out and grasped the chrome pole at the front of the deck and leaned outwards, swinging lazily around it, automatically hooking her legs up and snaking around in a sinuous arc.

She hadn't practised all summer. But she hadn't forgotten the moves.

Walking around the pole, she grasped it high up and stretched her legs out wide, twisting her body around and spinning gracefully to the ground. She repeated the move, this time curling around the pole in a foetal position, her knees tucked up. The music informed her movements—slow, indolent, but ripe with sensuality. Shinning to the top of the pole, she wrapped her thighs tightly around it, gasping in exquisite pain at the pressure of the cool chrome on her burning flesh. The memory of Angelo's hands on her waist as they danced last night filled her head, driving her to the brink of oblivion. Eyes closed, head tipped back in an agony of remembrance she spread her legs wide and swivelled down before climbing up again.

Her body pulsed with longing for his touch, the warmth of his breath on her neck. The music held her in thrall, throbbing through her as she let her body twist and curve almost of its own volition, every move an expression of desperate need. Dropping backwards in a sinuous arc, she gripped the pole near the floor and cartwheeled back to her feet as the music finished.

For a second there was silence.

Then Angelo's voice, cold and steel-edged.

'What the hell do you think you're doing?'

He was on the deck above, waiting for another call from London, when he heard the music. Recognizing it, he gave a wry smile as remembered sensations from last night crowded into his mind, driving out all thoughts of business.

He got up and walked over to the railing, leaning his back against it, reliving the dance. How long had they swayed together like that, oblivious to the rest of the world? Minutes? Hours? He didn't have a clue, he realised, and in his rigidly timetabled, efficiency-driven world that was unheard of. He'd let go of everything, in a way that was completely alien to him. He'd felt young. Carefree.

And Angelo Emiliani had never done young or carefree.

He couldn't afford to do them now either, he reflected ruefully, trying to re-focus his brain on the matters in hand. Countless phone calls to just about every contact in his address book had failed to come up with anything concrete on an Anna Field, and Ifford's solicitors were being extremely vague about when the contract on the château could be signed. French law dictated that the signatures of all interested parties had to be obtained, and it was taking some time to make the necessary arrangements. Angelo sneeringly assumed that the English aristocracy didn't work to the same imperatives as the rest of the business world.

Rubbing a hand over his eyes, he turned to look out over the serene ocean, and that was when the light from below caught his attention.

Or not the light, exactly. The shadow.

The lamps from the saloon spilled out on to the deck below, throwing a perfect silhouette of Anna on to the smooth boards, like a screen projection.

She was dancing.

Not just dancing… She was…

Dio mio…

It should have been sleazy, but it wasn't. Watching her, he was astonished by her graceful strength, by the smooth, elegant precision of her moves. She snaked around the pole with catlike neatness. Like a ballerina.

She'd surprised him again, he thought bleakly as the music came to an end. Surprised him and intrigued him, while all the time evading him. The girl was like a nuclear explosion in the centre of his well-ordered life.

'What the hell do you think you're doing?'

She scrambled to her feet, her chest rising and falling quickly, a thin sheen of sweat on her skin. Angelo crossed the deck with swift, savage strides. His face was as impassive as always—glacial in its calm—but she could see a muscle flicker in the lean plane of his jaw.

He stopped in front of her.

She tilted her chin defiantly, but behind her back her hands gripped the pole to stop her knees from giving way beneath her. The look in his eyes was blistering.

'I was bored.'

He gave an incredulous rasp of laughter and ran a hand through his unruly mane of gold.

'*Bored?*'

And then their mouths met and his hands were on the pole above her head, trapping her in a cage of his body. Her fists flew to his rock-hard chest, beating against the solid wall of muscle, while their tongues fought and meshed in the hot cavern of their mouths. She felt her hands slide round his back, her fingers helplessly kneading his silken flesh, her nails convulsively digging themselves into his skin.

Still he held on. Apart from his mouth, he wasn't touching her at all, his arms braced against the metal pole, his head bent to hers. But his kiss was hot, savage and full of hunger.

Suddenly she ducked under his arm, stooping low and swinging out from the pole as he had seen her do as she had danced. Straightening up on the other side, she looked at him with naked desire.

'Yes. *Bored.* You're always working.'

He took a step backwards and gave her a hard, appraising smile. His eyes glittered with lust.

'I have to try to stay one step ahead of you and your friends.'

Idly, slowly, lazily she shinned up the pole and swung around at the top, arching herself down towards him.

'You're wasting your time.'

'Am I?'

He reached out a hand and traced a languorous finger around her belly button, flicking the silver bar there, never taking his eyes off her face. He saw her eyes darken and her eyelids flutter at his touch and was ready for her as she shivered and faltered. Snaking an arm around her waist, he lifted her down. Her legs closed around his waist as tightly as they had gripped the pole, her strong dancer's muscles squeezing him.

'Well, maybe I shouldn't wast any more time, then,' he said harshly, carrying her through the saloon. His mouth was set in a grim line, his fingers hard on her ribs. She felt a delicious flutter of fear and anticipation as he kicked open the door to her cabin. He looked down at her for a moment, his expression dark and savage.

'I might not know who you are, Anna Field, but I know what you want.'

She whimpered. And then, almost without knowing how, her hands were in his hair, her mouth crashed and ground against his as he dropped her on the bed and tore at the fastening of his shorts. Her fingers closed around the back of his neck and she pulled him down beside her. Holding his face in both hands, she looked into his eyes with an expression that threatened to tip him over the edge of desire into total abandonment.

Her mouth closed over his again while her hands slid down the length of his arms to his wrists. Her fingers circled them in a steely grip as she hauled herself up so she was sitting on top of him. Without tearing her mouth from his, she edged her hips upwards until her knees rested on his outspread arms. The kiss deepened. They were tearing at each other's face with their mouths, grinding, rasping, devouring.

Then suddenly she threw her head backwards, gasping triumphantly. Her knees pinioned his arms to the bed on either side of him. Eyes glittering, she looked down on him.

'Got you' she whispered throatily.

He gazed up at her as a slow smile curved his bruised lips, making those little brackets at each corner of his mouth. Sinuously he edged downwards beneath her, so that her crotch was centimetres from his mouth.

He breathed out. Heavily.

She moaned as the heat of his breath fanned the fire raging through her pelvis and caressed her more intimately, more delicately, more thoroughly than she had thought possible. Her eyes closed in blissful submission, then flew open again as she felt the first stroke of his tongue.

'Oh, God. Oh—oh, Angelo—'

He felt the shudder that shook her whole body.

'Take them off,' he breathed.

Her hands went to her bikini bottoms and she rose up on her knees as she frantically tugged them downwards. He watched her, waiting for the moment when she would have to lift her knees to remove the tiny scrap of white fabric, and as she did so he flipped her over so she rolled on to the bed beneath him.

In one fluid movement he was astride her.

'Got *you*.'

She jerked and bucked under his thighs, half rising up on her elbows, wanting to fight, but wanting to surrender more. He inserted a knee between her hot, writhing thighs, separating her legs and spreading them wide open. Growling, snarling, she pushed her hips upwards, questing for the hardness of him that she could see but not touch, almost deranged with the need to feel him inside her.

Watching him slide on a condom was almost more than she could bear.

With one slow thrust he entered her, and felt a sudden shock, like lightning through his veins at the momentary look of vulnerability that passed across her face, the soft gasp that sprang from her sweet mouth. Surely she couldn't be...?

'Anna?'

He withdrew, and she let out a cry of pure desperation, arching her hips up towards him again. Her eyes locked into his, any trace of hesitation vanished in the blistering heat of her need. Sensing his uncertainty she pressed her fists against his chest, clawing, beating, every blow an expression of her longing. He thrust slowly into her again.

'Who are you?' he whispered harshly, almost despairingly.

Her eyes were a dark abyss from which she looked at him with hopeless desire.

'I don't know. I'm—oh, God—' He thrust into her again. 'I'm whatever...you want me...to be.'

He leaned forward, low over her face, brushing her lips with his as he withdrew again.

'Or everything I *don't* want you to be.'

He thrust into her again. Through a haze of ecstasy she looked up at him.

'That's...' she breathed out, closed her eyes and slid a hand around his neck, pulling his head down to hers so that her lips caressed his ear '...that's what you *like*. That's why I'm here.'

With a primitive growl he gathered her to his chest and then they were rolling and fighting and writhing together in a tangle of limbs and hands and mouths, until finally Anna arched her back and let out a shout of rapture that drifted across the dark ocean. In silent joy Angelo held her shuddering body and let go, feeling his own release like a triumph.

Her hair fanned out on the pillow, black and pink. He looked down at her, at her heart-shaped face, her flushed cheeks, her swollen mouth with its perfect Cupid's-bow lips smudged and reddened. Silently she looked back. Defiant, but defeated by her own need.

She must have slept, or at least fallen into that deeply relaxed state of total, contented submission. The next thing she knew Angelo was gently easing his arm out from beneath her head and tugging the sheet over her naked body.

'Hmm? What are you doing? Where are you going?'

He leaned over her, his perfect face as blank and pale as marble in the moonlight.

'I'm going back to my cabin.'

'No! Stay! You can't just leave like that, after we...after *that*.' She stretched out a hand towards him, suddenly bereft. He captured it and kissed her fingertips, then placed her hand softly down on the bed.

He stood upright, looking terrifyingly remote and heartbreakingly gorgeous.

She struggled into a sitting position, clutching the sheet to her breasts as she watched him walk towards the door.

'Angelo—' she called out, unable to stop herself.

He turned.

'Did I do something wrong?'

He shook his head, unsmiling.

'Sex is for sharing. But I sleep alone.'

And with that he was gone.

CHAPTER EIGHT

Opening her eyes, Anna found the cabin flooded with sunlight. She stretched luxuriously, feeling the pleasurable ache in her thighs, the delicious throb at their apex, then she frowned.

In spite of the brightness of the day, a shadow lurked at the edge of her mind. Her thoughts roved over the events of last night, to the point where Angelo had left her, and she felt a little flip in her stomach as she remembered his distance, his beauty.

God, he was amazing…

But that wasn't what was bothering her. If anything, his remoteness intrigued her. She respected it.

No, something else…

She got up and padded over the thick carpet into her *en suite* bathroom. In the mirror her face looked hopelessly young, but that vagueness, that vacuum that she often felt when she looked at herself was absent.

Who are you…? he had asked.

She closed her eyes and tipped her head back as the remembered words shivered through her consciousness. She had found somewhere where she felt she belonged. Here. Out in the middle of nowhere with this man who called up feelings and responses in her that she had never had before. That she had never even suspected she was capable of.

It felt as if this was what she had been born for.

Her eyes snapped open.

Oh, God, that was it. The shadow at the back of her thoughts. It was her birthday today.

Resolutely she stared at herself in the glass, holding tightly on to the edge of the basin. Her birthday, and the anniversary of her mother's death, when Lisette had been killed as she'd sped through the countryside, bringing back the cake she had ordered from the caterers for Anna's party. It had been the first summer they hadn't been at the château, as Lisette had decided that Anna should be at home and have a proper party for the girls from her school.

She'd been at St Catherine's for a term by then and had hated every minute of it. The lessons had bored her, the rules had horrified and confounded her and the other girls had teased her— delighting in provoking her fiery temper. Used to being an only child and perfectly happy in her own company, Anna had found the enforced proximity of the dormitories suffocating. She had been small and way behind the other girls, some of whom had already started wearing bras and talking about boys. Scared of showing her naiveté Anna had kept herself aloof from them, earning herself a reputation for being 'stuck-up'.

It hadn't been a good start.

Keen to improve matters before term started again in September, Lisette had planned a lavish party at Ifford, which Anna had been ferociously against. The thought of all her hated classmates coming to Ifford had filled her with utter horror. Ifford was huge and had once been extremely grand, but it had long since fallen into shabbiness. There had never been enough money to keep the rain out and the furnishings up to date and her parents were of the bohemian artistic persuasion that considered wall-to-wall carpets and videos and CD players to be completely irrelevant. Anna had known that her friends would find it all deeply pitiful, and had prayed fervently in the weeks leading up to the party for some surprise deliverance from the dreaded event.

She had got it.

Snatching up her toothbrush, she began to brush her teeth with savage thoroughness. Ten years ago. Of course she was old enough now not to blame herself, and to realize that she hadn't brought about the accident herself. Of course she was.

She stopped brushing.

But if only they had gone to the château as normal that year...

She thought of the wedding dress, still lying in the dusty attic, and felt tears prickle at the back of her eyes. It was almost as if a part of her refused to believe that Lisette was really gone, for ever, and that by hanging on to the château she might, somehow, find some way of turning the clock back and reversing that decision. Persuading Lisette out of the idea of the party. Spending another carefree summer swimming and dancing and inventing more games...

Keeping up the pretence that they were a normal family.

She spat toothpaste into the sink and rinsed out her mouth with water.

Twenty-one today, she thought desolately, and still dreaming of the impossible.

'I've found one.'

Angelo squinted into the sun and pressed the phone a little closer to his ear so he didn't miss what his PA was about to say.

'Go on, Helen.'

'Anna Field. Arrested in October 2003 for animal rights activities in Oxford, released with a caution.'

Angelo was very still. 'That sounds likely.'

'Lives in London,' Helen continued, 'works in a vegetarian café, aged forty-five, divorced—'

Angelo let out a single Italian expletive, which stopped Helen in her tracks. 'I'm sorry, Signor Emiliani, should I continue?'

The image of Anna's lithe, petite body winding itself around the pole last night swam in front of his eyes.

Again.

'No,' he snapped. 'It's not her. Not unless she's the most youthful forty-five-year-old on the planet. You're sure about the age?'

'Yes, *signor*. It's on her police records.'

'OK, well, keep looking. The solicitors in Nice are still waiting for Ifford to send someone to sign the papers, and the longer it takes the more chance these bloody eco-warriors have of complicating the whole process immeasurably.' He couldn't keep Anna on board indefinitely, however tempting that prospect seemed after her performance last night.

Precisely because of her performance last night... Who knew what might happen if he spent much longer with her?

Angelo switched the phone off and threw it down on to the cushioned deck couch beside him. He picked up the plain brown folder that was lying there and leaned back on one elbow to leaf through it.

Last night when he'd left Anna's cabin he'd come out here, as he often did, to work. He slept little, and badly, which he guessed went back to his days of sharing a room with twenty other children. Twenty other abandoned children, each with their own personal demons who visited nightly and made sure the hours of darkness were never peaceful.

Angelo had his own demons too, of course. Which was why he never slept with any of the women he bedded. As far as most people were concerned, sex would be the most intimate act two people could share, but to him, curling another person's body into his own and slipping into the oblivion of sleep was far, far more intimate and required a degree of trust that he didn't possess.

He couldn't leave himself so vulnerable in front of another human being. Lucia was the only person he had ever fallen asleep with—tiny, three-year-old Lucia, who'd been plagued by night terrors and asthma attacks. When she had first come to the orphanage she hadn't spoken for months and the only time anyone ever heard her voice was when she'd screamed in the night. Gradually, it had been Angelo who had won her trust—probably because he had been the one who had tried the least. When she used to creep into his bed in the night he had at first taken her back to her own little cot with its single rough blanket. But eventually he had relented and kept her with him—wrapping his own blanket around her, sitting with her propped up against him to ease her breathing, hardly slipping into sleep at all so that he would be able to lift her back into her own bed before the nuns rang the morning bell.

He realised he had been leafing through the sketches he had done last night without seeing them. Rubbing a hand over his stinging eyes, he looked again.

They were of the château, but they weren't businesslike architectural drawings showing proposed floor layouts and extension plans. They were impressions, memories of the building from when Anna had shown him round. Letting them come to rest on his chest, he lay back and sighed.

He wanted this property. Badly.

He'd wanted Anna too but, far from satisfying that need, possessing her had only made it stronger. *Gesù*, he thought bitterly, his first impression of her had been absolutely right. Whoever she was, she was toxic. She was fiery and surprising and addictive and contradictory—an eco-warrior who stayed on one of the Riviera's most opulent hotels, a pole dancer who was also a virgin. All of this might make her as intriguing as hell, but as far as he was concerned it also meant she was one hundred per cent bad news.

He needed her out of his life and out of his head so he could concentrate properly on this deal.

Anna trailed slowly up the steps to the sun deck. She was beginning to get very happily accustomed to life at sea, having been introduced to the hallowed sanctuary of the below-deck gym. Paulo had taken her there, saying with a slight smile, 'Signor Emiliani thought you might find this a more suitable place for a work-out, Signorina Field.'

Once her initial indignation had subsided, she had enjoyed herself hugely. She was no regular gym-bunny on land, but this was different. Gleaming white, totally secluded, there was a purity about the place that appealed to her and, selecting a soothing new-age soundtrack, she had lost herself in the simple release of physical exercise, emerging later feeling purged.

Her limbs felt as if they were filled with warm honey and her mind was pleasantly numb.

Rounding the corner at the front of the boat, she stopped sharply and, swearing curtly beneath her breath, took a step backwards again. For there, stretched out on the wide cushioned area that surrounded the hot tub, was Angelo.

She half turned, muttering, 'Sorry.' Then turned back.

He was asleep.

She hesitated, not wanting to approach him, not able to stop herself. Hardly breathing, she found herself stepping towards him on tiptoe, until she stood looking down on to his face.

She felt her breath escape in a long, awestruck exhalation. His hair fell back from his golden forehead, showing the darker layer underneath where the sun had not bleached it to white-goldness. His nose was so perfectly straight, his cheekbones hard and high, his mouth utterly composed and still.

But he looked different. With those startling, penetrating eyes closed, his face had lost its cold, amused air and looked simply young and heartbreakingly beautiful. Tilting her head to one side, she smiled, remembering her surprise at how young he was when she'd first met him at the château. He was surely barely older than the boys she knew in London who shared squalid bachelor flats with each other and got drunk and groped girls on Friday nights.

She laughed softly.

This man…this man…was in a different league.

Her eyes travelled downwards slowly, as her throat constricted with desire. He was like a Renaissance sculpture cast in gold—perfectly proportioned, utterly flawless. Biting her lip, she let her gaze skim over the lean planes of his stomach, frustratingly obscured by the sheaf of papers he held against him. Gently she reached out, telling herself she was only acting in his best interests. He'd be furious if he woke up to find his tan was marred by a large A4-shaped paler patch… Carefully, so as not to wake him, she extracted them from his loose grip and looked round for somewhere to put them.

She glanced down at them and felt a tiny *frisson* of shock as she recognized the familiar outline of Château Belle-Eden, sensitively brought to life in a few masterful strokes of black ink. Quickly she leafed though the sketches—the front elevation, with its familiar gables and turrets, the French windows from the salon which led down a flight of stone steps into the rose garden—all of it drawn with such skill and clarity that it brought tears to her eyes. She almost felt she could peer more closely into the picture and see her mother's piano through the French windows, and beyond it the staircase with her ten-year-old self descending in that tattered white dress…

Oh, Mama, if only…

The next moment she was falling as an arm snaked around her waist and pulled her down on to the cushioned deck, scattering the papers. In one lithe movement Angelo rolled over and got up, towering above her as she lay, winded and shocked.

'Bad luck, Anna,' he said huskily. 'They're just sketches. No information. No plans. No details. You don't think I'd be stupid enough to leave anything significant lying around while you're here, do you?'

'I could see what they were,' she snapped, sitting up. 'I wasn't looking for anything. I was trying to—' His coldness and lack of trust stung her, so she couldn't think straight. 'Oh, never mind,' she muttered miserably, getting to her feet. 'As a matter of fact, I was just thinking how lovely they were.' She bent and picked up the picture of the French windows, looking down at it for a moment, before thrusting it at him. 'But then it is an exceptionally lovely building, which is precisely why we intend to protect it from the same fate as that house you showed me yesterday.'

'*Protect* it?' Angelo walked away from her, speaking slowly, his voice dripping with scorn. He hadn't slept for long, but during that brief spell of unconsciousness he had dreamed disjointedly of Lucia and his earlier frustration had hardened into a smouldering anger. He shook his head disbelievingly at Anna's careless words. 'And can you explain to me exactly why a *building* needs protection? Anna, the world is full of suffering and injustice and you choose to devote your time to *protecting* a *building*.'

She looked at him, hurt and pride welling in her wide eyes.

'Yes, well, at least I'm doing something worthwhile instead of just accumulating indecent sums of money by committing acts of hideous vandalism on national architectural treasures. Buildings need protecting for posterity, for future generations to enjoy.'

He had turned away from her, but she could see the tension in his broad brown shoulders as he thrust a hand through his hair. Her heart lurched uncomfortably in her chest, but whether it was out of fear for what he was about to say or the persistent nagging undercurrent of sickening desire she felt when she looked at him she couldn't tell.

'Future generations? I see. That would be future generations of the wealthy, idle, privileged families who have already enjoyed them for hundreds of years, would it?'

Families who put land, titles, a name, *for pity's sake, before the welfare of their own children.*

'Maybe. What does that matter if they're being looked after by people who care about them and the land that surrounds them? This isn't just about bricks and mortar, it's about land and how it's managed and maintained in the same way as it's been for centuries—without bulldozing woodland to make way for executives to land their Learjets!'

He spun round slowly. His narrow eyes were penetratingly blue, his mouth eloquently communicating his utter scorn. '*Land?* You environmentalists are just as bad as the nuns in the convent where I grew up. You genuinely believe that you're acting for some sort of higher authority, for the common good, but you're so blinkered by your own piety, so *blinded* by your own virtue that you can't see what's really going on around you. You feel so passionately about this building, Anna, and about its *land…* You really think you and your scruffy, irresponsible friends are striking some huge blow for democracy and perpetuity, but you couldn't be more pitifully misguided.'

He had taken a step towards her and was standing very close. His tone was lazy, but that just made the venom of his words all the more powerful. Anna felt the blood drain from her face.

'How…how dare you…?'

'Because it's the truth. You'd like everything to stay the same, would you? For *posterity*? Lovely idea, Marie-Antoinette, but may I suggest you wake up and take a long hard look at the real world. It's not all picture-book castles and fairy-tale princesses, it's poverty and disease and injustice. It's about ruthless self-interest. About people sacrificing other, more vulnerable people for their own purposes. You can't see past the romantic ideal that the château symbolizes, but the reality is that the history of buildings like that represents a whole lot of misery and exploitation. Of the lower orders. Of women and…and *children*, for God's sake, of people forced into rigid roles and restricted and repressed. I *free* buildings from all that. I don't protect them, I make them *relevant*. You're just too immature to see that.'

Ouch.

She looked down. Anything to avoid the chilling contempt on his face, but he had already moved away and was putting the sketches back into their folder.

Tears prickled dangerously at the back of her eyes, but she was determined not to let them fall. Desperately attempting to sound utterly unemotional, she said, 'If you've quite finished, I'd like to go. I want you to take me back to shore.'

'Of course. We're headed back to Cannes now.'

'Good. It was stupid of me to come. I don't know what I was thinking of.'

That's good. Make it all sound like nothing more than a tedious interlude. An unfortunate error of judgement. Nothing personal.

'I don't think you were thinking at all. But, if you were, I imagine it was about what you could gain from coming.'

Her cool façade cracked. 'What's that supposed to mean?'

'Information about what I intend to do with the château,' he said reasonably, coming back towards her. 'But, more immediately, sex.'

'You...*you bastard*. You wanted it as much as I did!'

He looked at her thoughtfully and slid a finger down her midriff, circling the diamond bar. 'I wanted it, that's true. But you wanted it more.'

There was a second's silence. Then the sharp crack of her hand as it made stinging contact with his cheek.

He hardly moved. Had it not been for the bright blossoming of colour that spread across his cheekbone, she would have thought she had barely touched him, but his eyes burned with icy rage. It seemed like an eternity that they held her. Anna's breath came in ragged gasps as she looked defiantly back up at him, every vein pulsing with adrenalin and fury.

And then he simply turned and walked away, without looking back. And Anna found that all her anger disappeared with him, leaving her feeling a miserable, churning desire and a sickening sense of self-loathing and shame.

Going back to her cabin, she started shivering so hard her teeth chattered as the full impact of the encounter hit her like a series of hammer-blows to her heart and her pride. Underneath the awfulness of feeling his anger and contempt like that, the worst thing was that she knew he was right.

She had wanted him more than she had ever wanted anyone before. Perhaps more than she had ever wanted anything too.

Apart from the château, she told herself fiercely. Her priority when she had come aboard the yacht had been finding out anything that would help GreenPlanet oppose his plans. Hadn't it?

But, as she lay curled up on the bed, shaking with shock and misery, she relived that searing lust she had felt when she'd danced with him on the beach and knew that she wasn't being honest with herself.

Oh, God, he was right about everything.

GreenPlanet was a way of life and when she'd met Gavin and the rest of the group she'd been desperately seeking an escape from a home in which she felt she no longer belonged, and revenge on a family who had tried to pretend she was someone she wasn't.

She'd lost her future when she'd had to give up dancing, and she'd lost her past when she'd found out about her birth, and GreenPlanet had offered a perfect escape—a complete lifestyle package, where all the thinking was done for her. It *was* like a religion. It told her who to believe and what to do—even what to eat and what to wear. She had been so grateful for its direction that she'd never bothered to question the legitimacy of its creed, until now. And it scared her.

But Angelo's words scared her more. He had put his elegant finger exactly on the place in her heart where the hurt still welled and throbbed.

Hadn't her family sacrificed her, in a way, for the title? The Delafield bloodline? They'd tried to keep the truth hidden to preserve her father's pride and the purity of their oh-so-important heritage and family honour, but in doing so had left her with a deep, abiding sense of shame and self-loathing.

She was supposed to suffer the pain in silence, keep her scars hidden, play her part with nobility and grace. Mix with the right people, marry the right man and fill Ifford Park with children to perpetuate the name and continue the miserable charade. History would forget her own accident of birth.

Her own feelings were unimportant.

No!

Angelo was right. Her belief in the sanctity of the past was pathetically naïve, just as her wholehearted acceptance of the GreenPlanet ideology was spectacularly misguided. But what did that leave her with? Without a family identity, without dancing, without GreenPlanet, who was she?

She had been so busy rejecting all her father's values that she'd forgotten to get any of her own. So imprisoned in the past she'd forgotten to think about the future. So ashamed of who she wasn't she'd forgotten to find out who she really was. She even tried to deny she had a birthday.

From now on, she thought, pulling the duvet back and crawling beneath it like a wounded animal, this is my *re*-birthday. The day I learned enough about myself to realize I had to make a new start. For that, at least, she had Angelo to thank, and every birthday she would remember him.

Yeah right. And the other three hundred and sixty-four days of the year as well.

Much later, when the room was filled with violet shadow, there was a discreet knock at the door and Paulo appeared.

'Signor Emiliani asked me to tell you we'll be mooring in about an hour. I'll come and get you when he's ready to go ashore, *signorina*. In the meantime, is there anything I can get you?'

'No. No, thank you.'

So this was it. Time to say goodbye.

CHAPTER NINE

TWENTY minutes later Anna stepped out of the bath and reached for one of the vast thick towels to wrap around herself.

She had washed her hair and soaped every inch of herself thoroughly, partly to fill the time and partly in an attempt to be practical. If she was going to spend the next few days travelling she didn't know when she would next get the chance of a hot bath.

And a hot bath like this? Never.

Bending to wrap her hair in another towel, she straightened up and looked around her. The oval bath was sunk into a raised marble platform and surrounded by dark polished wood that Anna was certain was neither reclaimed nor from a sustainable source. The room, like the rest of the yacht, gave an impression of devil-may-care luxury, as if its designer could have required the very last trees in the forest for some minor embellishment and wouldn't have cared. Out of sheer habit, she found herself wondering what Gavin would make of it, and stopped herself.

She was going to learn to form her own judgements.

She loved it. And the contrast with the ancient clanking plumbing and draughty bathrooms at Ifford Park could hardly have been greater.

Padding back into the bedroom, she dismally surveyed her wardrobe choices and sighed. She was beginning to hate the sight of the denim hotpants and that damned white bikini. If only she hadn't been so quick to discard Fliss's dress at the beach party…

Memories rushed in and she smiled ruefully to herself. If she hadn't, maybe she wouldn't be here. She could have spared herself the heartache, but would also have missed out on the most significant thing to happen to her in years. The last two days had taught her so much. About sex for a start. But also about herself. Things she hadn't even begun to know before.

Her capacity for arousal, for enjoyment. And self-delusion.

Giving herself a mental shake, she dragged her attention back to the matter in hand. Clothes. Maybe she should have taken up Angelo's offer of something left behind by one of his previous visitors to the yacht. She imagined a closet full of gossamer wisps of designer fabric, scented with the perfume of other women, each one with its own memories and associations of which she would be oblivious but Angelo would be all too aware.

No, she couldn't have done that. Her time with him was all too brief as it was. At the very least she could know that he had been thinking of her while they had been together, not one of his many other women.

Dropping the towel to the floor, she slipped on the wretched bikini bottoms and picked up Angelo's shirt. Pressing the soft linen against her face, she could still discern the faintest trace of his scent.

That would soon fade, like she would from his memory.

Briskly she did up the buttons and regarded herself dismally in the mirror. She wanted to make an impression on him as she left, make him admire her poise and sophistication and maturity. Instead she looked like a schoolgirl. Her hair, tangle free and straight, fell down past her shoulders in a dark silky waterfall, obscuring the streaks of pink. The sun had tanned her skin to a deep olive brown and her eyes, without their usual dark smudging of kohl, looked wide and vulnerable.

She was hardly going to attract more than a cursory glance from him like this.

Looking around, she caught sight of Fliss's little sequinned evening scarf on the back of a chair and tied it round her hips in a desperate attempt to make it look as if she wasn't dressed for bed. It made the shirt rather shorter, displaying a little bit more of her long tanned thighs than she was comfortable with, but she pushed her doubts away.

She was hardly dressed to kill. She'd be lucky to inflict even minor injury. But it was the best she could do. She jumped at the knock on her cabin door.

'Signor Emiliani is waiting, *signorina*. If you'd like to follow me?'

Now she had to go out there and hold her head high while she said goodbye to the man who had changed her life.

The sky had darkened to a quiet indigo-rose. Stepping out on to the deck, Anna felt the caress of the warm sea-scented air on her bare legs and blinked.

It was so quiet.

She looked around in confusion, searching for some familiar landmark from which she could get her bearings. Instead she found her gaze coming to rest on Angelo.

He was leaning against the deck rail, dressed in faded jeans and a dark blue T-shirt, and he straightened up as she approached. Across the darkening space between them, his eyes met hers and held them.

She felt her pulse surge and her stomach tighten. Desperate not to show him how much she wanted him, she frowned.

'Where are we? This isn't Cannes…'

He took a step towards her, sliding his hands into the pockets of his jeans, dipping his head and looking at her from under his hair. Newly washed, it was white-gold and tousled. Her fingers itched with the longing to touch it.

'No. We're not far away—St Honorat.' She recognized the name of the tiny island just off the coast. 'I wanted to apologize for this afternoon before you left. I said some harsh things.'

Anna straightened her spine and lifted her head to meet his gaze squarely. 'There's no need. You were absolutely right,' she said stiffly. Unable to look at him any longer, she turned her face to the sea, letting the warm breeze whip her hair across her cheeks, giving her a welcome curtain to hide behind. 'Please don't feel you have to waste any more of your precious time on me. You've lost two days already.'

'I don't think they could be called entirely wasted,' he drawled softly, reaching out his hand. She closed her eyes. *Please don't touch me. Please don't be nice or I won't be able to stop myself from crying, or kissing you, or telling you I—'*

She felt his fingers close around her chin, turning her head towards him with infinite gentleness. She kept her eyes fixed on the floor as she spoke, desperately trying to keep the tremor out of her voice. 'It's been…fun,' she finished lamely, as misery washed over her.

'Fun? You have a very odd idea of fun, Anna Field. But it's not over yet.'

She glanced sharply up at him. Eyes glittering with amusement, he stood aside and swept an arm in the direction of the shore behind him.

'Dinner?'

She gasped. A crescent of deserted beach stretched out on both sides, and in the mauve twilight she could see candles glittering around a blanket spread out on the silver sand. 'Wh—what do you mean? I can't—I mean, I shouldn't. I have to get back to Cannes, I—'

He sighed, taking her hand and lacing his long fingers though hers.

'You really are the most contrary, difficult, rebellious girl I've ever met. Do you realize how idiotic I'm going to look in front of my crew if I have to ask them to pack all that away and sail on to Cannes now? Not to mention the irresponsibility of letting all that food go to waste.'

His tone was light and mocking, but the touch of his hand was sending X-rated messages right to the core of her. Trying to control the dizzying waves of desire that lapped through her, she pulled her hand away. Blushing, she mumbled, 'I probably can't eat it anyway. I'm vegetarian.'

'Do you think I hadn't worked that out?'

'I'm not dressed…'

'What's new?'

'I—'

'Stop arguing. Come on.'

The long wooden jetty that stretched from the beach to the yacht tender was too narrow to walk along side by side, so Angelo let Anna go in front of him. A mistake, he thought wryly, unable to take his eyes off her long bare legs. She looked sensational—relaxed and soft and almost unrecognizable from the wary, aggressive girl he had met at the château. She seemed different too, he mused silently. Quieter, more subdued. More grown up somehow. Maybe removing her from the influence of those hippy wasters had done her a favour.

Their bare feet sank into the soft sand as they reached the end of the jetty and she hesitated, looking round at him. A light sea breeze caught her hair so it streamed back from her face, showing the streaks of pink.

'It's beautiful.'

He smiled. 'I was just thinking the same thing,' he said lightly, taking her hand. She was trembling, he realized with a slight lurch inside his chest. All of a sudden she seemed very young and vulnerable.

Dammit.

This was his last chance, he reminded himself as he led her

across the uneven sand towards the cashmere rug his crew had laid out and weighed down with heavy stones. All around they'd set hurricane lanterns containing thick church candles, and had left a basket containing the picnic and a silver bucket containing a bottle of vintage champagne and one of local *rosé* nestling in ice.

They'd done well.

He'd spent the last two days exploring all the avenues he could think of, trying to find out exactly who this girl was and what she was up to, and he'd come up against dead end after dead end. It had been partly frustration that had made him lose it so spectacularly this afternoon. Afterwards he'd realized he had missed the very thing that had been right under his nose all this time.

Her.

He'd been so busy fighting with her it hadn't occurred to him to get the answers to everything he wanted to know straight, as it were, from the horse's mouth.

He handed her a couple of glasses and slid the bottle out of the ice bucket. Easing the cork out with his thumbs, he held it aloft as a plume of foam cascaded out and splashed over her feet, making her gasp.

He looked directly into her eyes, noticing the blush that spread across her cheeks in the soft evening light. Easy. This was going to be easy.

She held out the glasses and, without taking his eyes from hers, he splashed champagne into them. It spilled over, running down her arms.

He took one of the glasses from her and with his other hand picked up her wrist and held it to his mouth, running his tongue along the rivulet of champagne, to her elbow.

'To getting to know each other,' he said softly.

The champagne bubbles sparkled against her tongue, but that was nothing to the rocket-bursts of shooting stars that exploded in the pit of her stomach as his warm mouth moved down the inside of her arm. She gritted her teeth against the ecstasy that threatened to erupt from her in a whimper of pleasure.

'What's the point of getting to know each other?' she rasped. 'We're about to say goodbye.'

He lifted his head and gave her a smile that went straight to her knees.

'Ah, come on, Anna. You're not making this easy. I've behaved like a pig, and this is my way of making amends. We've become pretty well acquainted in some ways over the last couple of days, but I'm aware I don't really know the first thing about you.'

'But that was never part of the deal, was it, Angelo?' Anna took a few steps away from him and turned to look out over the sea so he couldn't see the pain in her eyes. The lights of the yacht reflected on the flat silky water and it was almost impossible to tell where the sky began and the sea ended. 'You took me on to the yacht because you wanted to *change* my mind, not become intimately acquainted with it. Anyway—' she sighed '—I don't know why you're suddenly suffering an attack of conscience. I bet you hardly bother to ask the names of most of the women you sleep with. There's absolutely no need to make an exception for me.'

For a long moment all that could be heard was the soft sigh of the ocean. And then he spoke and in the warm twilight his voice was rough and low.

'It was your first time. I think that makes it exceptional. And did it occur to you that I might just want to make an exception for you?'

She turned slowly round. The candlelight turned his skin to burnished gold and emphasized the deep hollows beneath his hard, high cheekbones. He was looking at her steadily, his face for once not showing any signs of mockery or amusement. Her blood seemed suddenly to have been replaced with warm syrup.

She tore her eyes away from him and shook her head.

'No. I don't believe you. You hate everything I stand for. You hate everything about me.'

Very gently she felt the glass being taken from her hand. He put them both down, then took her hands in his. 'Anna, Anna, Anna, does the word paranoid mean anything to you? I confess, on paper we're hardly soul mates—'

'That has to be the understatement of the century. I'm a member of the environmental action group that intends to put a stop to your development of the château, Angelo. Let's not pretend we can be friends.'

'We've been lovers.'

'No. We've had sex. I think there's a difference.'

He laughed, but it was tinged with irony 'You're right, of course, but maybe I'd like to make up for that. I should have shown a little more restraint last night, but I must confess I had no idea you were a virgin.' He tucked a strand of pink hair behind her ear and smiled ruefully. 'Which just goes to prove my point—we need to get to know each other a little better. Look, I confess that environmental activists aren't amongst my favourite people, but it could be worse… When I saw you at the hotel I had a sudden horrible thought that you might be some spoilt little rich girl with a title and a trust fund.'

She felt the blood freeze in her veins. 'That would be worse?' she said flatly.

'Much worse. Now…' He put a finger under her chin and tilted her face up to his. 'Either you relax and stop behaving as if you're being force fed toads, or I'll…' he hesitated, his mouth curving into a wicked half-smile '…I'll have to do something about it.'

'You could try,' she said coldly, tugging her hands from his. 'But I don't like being told what to do, Angelo. Look, I really think we should just go—oh!'

In one deft movement he had swept her up into his arms and

was holding her against his chest. 'Angelo, what are you doing? Let me go! Put me down, *now*!'

'No. Not until you accept my apology and stop sulking. Otherwise—' he had begun to walk towards the sea, crossing the soft sand with long, loping strides '—you may just find yourself taking another dip.'

'No!' she squealed. 'No, Angelo, please! I haven't any more clothes!'

He stopped, and she felt the deep rumble of laughter within his chest. 'Is that supposed to put me off?'

Looking up, she could see the lean outline of his jaw, the hollow at the base of his throat. Her mouth suddenly felt very dry.

'Put me down,' she croaked.

He looked down into her face. 'Are you going to be a good girl?'

God. The look in his eyes sent a tidal wave of lust smashing through her, breaking down every flimsy defence and barrier and inhibition.

'No,' she whispered hoarsely, with a gasp that was meant to have been a laugh.

He whirled around, making her shriek and thrash in his arms as the world spun and only the hardness of his chest was real and solid.

'Stop! Stop, Angelo!' She felt dizzy and breathless with laughter.

He stopped, looking down at her with a deliberately deadpan expression. 'Are you going to be nice and polite now, Anna, or shall I…?'

'No!' she squealed. 'Don't you dare…!'

'Are you going to be good?' His mouth was inches from her own. Gradually she stopped thrashing in his arms and in the sudden stillness felt the torment of a desire that needed to be sated. Soon.

'No,' she breathed. 'I don't want to be a good girl. I want to be very, very naughty.'

His mouth came down on hers and the breaking of the waves was drowned out by the sound of the blood crashing through her veins. He was still holding her against him, so she could feel the heat of his skin through their clothes, the hardness of his body. Dimly she was aware that he was walking back up the beach with her, but she was lost in a world of flesh and fire, where the undulation of his stomach against her hip-bone spoke of something far more intimate. She felt him stoop, felt the softness of the rug beneath her, then he was standing over her, his eyes dark and unreadable.

She writhed, arching her back upwards, pulled towards him by invisible cords of instinctive longing. 'Angelo...you can't just stop...'

He laughed softly and lowered himself on to the rug beside her, languidly leaning over to the picnic basket beside them. 'Now, listen here, Anna Field or whoever you are. I can do what I like because I'm the host of this party and you're the guest, and you're supposed to be behaving yourself.'

He pulled out boxes and began to open them. Anna lay back and gazed up at the sky. Dark lilac and velvety and scattered with a million brilliant stars, it was as beautiful and opulent as a designer dress.

'Do you eat fish?'

She was about to say no—like all the other GreenPlanet members she'd been a strict, label-reading, nothing-with-a-face-on vegetarian. But suddenly she didn't care. She loved fish.

'Yes. I think tonight I eat just about anything.'

'Good. Close your eyes.'

Rolling over on to her side and propping herself up on one elbow, she looked at him. In the soft flickering light he looked like a young prince from one of the fairy-tale books she used to adore as a child.

'Anna,' he said with mock warning, 'do as you're told or I swear I'll...'

'OK! They're closed!'

She waited, her senses on high alert, her breathing fast and shallow, a giggle rising irrepressibly in her chest.

Something brushed against her lips. She opened them, questing, wanting, and bit down on something soft and delicious. Langoustine.

'Mmm…more.'

'Good girl.' His voice was very close to her ear, his breath caressing her neck. She opened her mouth again and was rewarded with another bite of fragrant langoustine, this time dipped in cool, creamy mayonnaise.

She groaned, lost in deep, greedy, sensuous pleasure.

'Good girl, that's better.'

She let her eyes drift open. His head was bent and the sun-bleached gold of his hair looked almost white in the candlelight. She slowly levered herself up into a sitting position and reached for her champagne. Taking a long mouthful, she leaned over and pressed her lips to his, filling his mouth with cool liquid silk.

A drop ran down her chin as they pulled apart.

'This isn't supposed to be happening like this,' he said hoarsely. 'We're supposed to be getting to know each other.'

'We are.'

'Not like this. We've introduced ourselves this way already.'

'So ask me a question.'

Who are you?

Angelo pushed the thought away. *Slowly. Don't rush her. Don't scare her.* Picking up another delicate curled langoustine, he dipped it into the mayonnaise and offered it to her quivering lips.

'What's your favourite colour?'

She leaned back on her elbows and looked at him consideringly. 'I don't know. Black.'

He rolled his eyes and gave her a stern look. 'You have to be sensible. Honest answers only. Or you have to do a forfeit.'

She laughed, and it was such a sweet, happy, musical sound that it took him by surprise.

'How will you know if I'm being honest?'

'You forget, *tesoro*,' he growled, 'that I have carved out a business and an extremely large fortune on instinct alone. I can tell when you're lying. Now, what's your favourite colour?'

'Pink'

'Good girl.' He held out another prawn, watching with satisfaction as her plump pink lips closed around its soft flesh. 'Middle name.'

She groaned. 'Josephine. After my French grandmother.'

Angelo felt a tiny dart of triumph. *Good. Carefully now. Keep going.*

'Best subject at school?'

She wiped mayonnaise off her lip. 'None of them. I hated school with a passion. I suppose I hated games marginally less than everything else. Look, shouldn't I be asking you some questions as well?'

'Go on, then.'

She hesitated, suddenly shy. 'Where are you from?'

'Milan.' He spoke abruptly.

'And did you…' She faltered and started again. 'You said something this afternoon about being brought up by nuns. What did you mean?'

'I was brought up in a convent orphanage.'

'I see.' She kept her head down and didn't look at him or attempt to touch him. *Interesting*, thought Angelo wryly. He could count on the fingers of one hand the number of women he had told about his childhood, but all of them had reacted in the same way—with suffocating affection, as if their kisses could somehow make up for those years.

'Your turn, I think.' She was looking at him over the rim of her champagne glass. He reached over for the bottle and topped it up, more to distract him from his unsettling thoughts than because she needed it.

'Where did you learn to dance like that?'

She slanted him a wicked glance from under sooty eyelashes. 'Like what?'

'Like you danced last night,' he replied gruffly, not wanting to let his mind take him back there. *Focus.*

She sighed, suddenly sad. 'I was training to be a ballet dancer, but I had a problem with the bones in my ankle. There was a weakness—the doctors didn't know why. I had an operation, which was successful enough, but I had to give up ballet. Pole dancing was a substitute. It uses lots of the same skills, the same muscles and strength in the legs but doesn't involve too much pressure on the feet.'

He leaned over and picked up her foot, tracing his thumb over the inch-long scar on the inside of her ankle, frowning in the gathering dusk as he steeled himself to ask the question that was forming on his lips. This could be the key.

It was *business.*

'Where did you do your ballet training?'

'Uh-uh.' She shook her head seriously. 'My turn. Favourite food.'

'Hmm…' he said, wondering why he felt a tingle of relief. 'Difficult. Food is wonderful. *Can* be wonderful,' he corrected himself. 'The food when I was growing up was appalling. But now I love dark, bitter chocolate, and figs, and really good bread, and Parma ham, and these…' He picked up a langoustine and put it in his mouth. 'I can't choose just one.'

'And, let me guess, you feel the same about your women too?' she said lightly, taking a sip of champagne.

'Absolutely. Now, my question. How old are you?'

'Twenty. No—twenty-one.'

Topping up his own glass, he paused and raised an eyebrow. 'You're not sure?'

'It's my birthday. Today,' she said quietly.

Contrition sliced through him like a razor. *Benedetto Gesù,* here he was playing mind games with her when she should be with her friends, having a party, celebrating. Twenty-one. *Bloody, bloody hell.*

'I'm sorry.' He got up stiffly and packed away the box that had contained the prawns and the mayonnaise.

'Why?' Her voice was leaden.

'I've kept you from your friends. That was wrong. You should have said; I would never have suggested—'

'It's all right. I hadn't planned to do anything. I don't like birthdays much. So this…' she looked around at the beach, the candles, him… 'this is…nice. Now,' she added hastily, desperately trying to rekindle the relaxed mood, 'my question. Do you have any brothers or sisters?'

He stopped what he was doing and suddenly went very still.

'No. Not that I know of. Except that I—Sort of.'

He rubbed a hand over his eyes. Great. Very articulate. What the hell was wrong with him all of a sudden? He had started this stupid thing for completely practical reasons. This was work. *Just answer her questions and choose your own very carefully*, he berated himself. *Concentrate.*

'Angelo?'

She was standing behind him, a little distance away. He turned. In the dim light her small heart-shaped face was full of anxiety. 'Tell me…'

'There's nothing to tell,' he said harshly, taking out a package of fragrant bread and a covered dish containing artichoke hearts, sun-dried tomatoes and olives glistening in oil. 'I don't know who my parents are. I was handed in at a convent somewhere in the South of France when I was a few hours old. From there I was taken to the foundling orphanage in Milan. They called me Angelo because I had blond hair, like an angel—' his voice was heavy with sarcasm, thinly disguising the hurt '—and gave me the surname Emiliani because St Jerome Emiliani is the patron saint of abandoned children.'

There was a small silence, filled by the silky rustle of the sea.

'You have no idea who your parents were?'

He hesitated, thinking of the ruby and diamond earring he kept in a box in his safe. The Paris jeweller he had shown it to had been able to tell him it was made by Cartier in 1922 and was almost certainly unique. From that information it would probably have been possible to discover the name of the original purchaser, but he hadn't done so. It would tell him either that his mother was some rich aristocrat who valued her family name above the welfare of her child, or that she was a common thief. Of the two, he would definitely have chosen the latter.

'No. I was wrapped in a shawl made of cashmere and there was a pretty expensive piece of jewellery tucked inside, so I assume my mother wasn't pushed for money,' he said acidly. 'My guess is she was from one of those backgrounds where an illegitimate child would have meant exclusion from all the best parties of the season.'

He waited for her to say what people always said. *I'm sorry.* Stupid, inadequate words that would mean he would have to smile and say, *It's fine.* But the silence stretched and deepened.

'Children live such terrible lives,' she whispered. 'I think we forget, as adults, how awful it can be to be helpless, and alone, and at the mercy of things you can't control.'

'Was your life awful?'

'No. No.'

'But?'

'But…nothing. You said you had "sort of" brothers and sisters. The other children in the orphanage?'

He gritted his teeth. *Gesù.* How the hell had he come to find himself talking about this? Never, not once in the last twelve years, had he uttered a single word about Lucia to anybody. But to deny her now would be an intolerable betrayal.

'One in particular,' he said curtly. 'A little girl called Lucia.'

Anna said nothing, just waited quietly for him to go on. God, he thought bleakly, why couldn't she just make it easier for him and fill the gap with inane chatter like any other woman would? He swallowed.

'She wasn't my real sister, of course, but she got very attached to me. I was sixteen, and she used to ask if she could come and live with me when I was old enough to leave, and if I could adopt her as my sister. I promised I would. It was what first motivated me to earn money—so I could get her out of there.'

He balled his hands into fists and with iron self-control held back the emotion that threatened to choke him. Glancing up, he could see the shimmer of tears in her dark eyes and almost succumbed. He stood up and, picking up a pebble from the sand, hurled it down towards the incoming tide.

'Anyway. She died. She had an asthma attack in the night. I wasn't there at the time and no one else heard. She was only three.'

For a long moment he stood, his back towards her, his shoulders tense. Then he turned and sat back down beside her, his emotions tightly reined in again, and managed a grim smile. 'So. My question, I think. Which do you prefer? Strawberries or grapes?'

Lying back on the rug, Anna sighed with contentment as Angelo packed the boxes back into the picnic basket.

If only she could freeze time, right here, for ever.

They had shared the food, taking it from each other's fingers, until there was nothing left but a few strawberries, and she felt replete.

Leaving only the more primeval hunger at the top of her thighs to be satisfied.

Her eyelids fluttered open a little; she wondered where Angelo was. Through the soft darkness she could just make out the outline of his broad shoulders down by the water's edge, and she felt her heart lurch as she watched him.

Tonight had been heaven. But tomorrow would be hell.

No. Don't think about it. Don't do what you always do and spoil it, don't push him away to try to defend yourself from getting hurt. This is your one chance, your one night. Savour every moment.

She got up and stretched, then began to walk down the beach towards him. The champagne and food had made her sleepy and languid, but there was a slow-burning need within her to be near him, to feel and taste and smell the scent of him.

'What are you doing?'

'Washing the oil off my hands. I don't want to leave finger-marks all over you.' He straightened up. 'Look what I found.'

He held out his hand and uncurled his fingers. Lying on his palm was a small pale shell, hinged in the middle, the two halves making a perfect heart shape.

'Oh,' she breathed, 'it's so pretty, so delicate.'

His eyes burned into hers as he took the shell and slipped it into the breast pocket of the shirt she was wearing. His hands were wet with salt water and icy drops fell on to the thin fabric, soaking through and making her gasp. Instantly she felt her nipple harden and as he took his hand away it brushed against his hot skin.

His face, inches from hers, was unreadable in the darkness, but above the whisper of the waves she thought she heard him moan quietly. The tiny sound tipped her over the edge into the yawning chasm of her desire. She was aware of her fingers, twisting themselves into the soft fabric of his T-shirt, pulling him to her, her lips seeking his, a soft pleading sound escaping her as they found his, and parted.

'No.'

The word brought her up short.

Angelo pulled away.

'Not like that. Not this time…' With something that felt like tenderness, he scooped her up in his arms and started to carry her back up the beach. His breathing was laboured, his voice low and grave as he set her gently down.

'No fighting this time. This time I want you to relax, to take it slowly…'

'God, Angelo…' her words were like a sob '…I don't know if I can… I want you so…'

He stopped her by planting a gossamer-light kiss on her lips. 'Shh…just relax…trust me…'

And with wonderful, agonizing, exquisite care he began to undo the buttons of her shirt. Looking upwards, Anna gazed in silent rapture at the infinite heavens, the vast, complicated miracle of the constellations, until, quivering with ecstasy and violent longing, her eyes slid out of focus and she was aware of nothing but her own private paradise.

CHAPTER TEN

IT WAS in the violet hour before dawn that Anna awoke.

Opening her eyes slowly, she saw the stars fading above her in a lavender sky and heard the distant sigh of the sea. Her cheeks felt cold, but beneath the blanket Angelo's body was wrapped around hers, warming her, shielding her from the chill morning air. For a second she closed her eyes and savoured the feeling of his arms around her, his long thighs tucked beneath her knees, his chest, reassuringly solid, rising and falling steadily against the curve of her back.

He had slept with her.

A tiny glow of joy flickered somewhere in the darkness of her heart. When she had gone, in the bleak days and nights—the bleak years—that lay ahead, she would always have that. It wasn't much, but it was something that she had shared with him that he had given no one else.

She half regretted that she had slept at all, but in the afterglow of their lovemaking she had been exhausted. And it was a final giving, one last intimacy after all that their bodies had shared with each other.

She looked down. His hand lay, fingers loosely curled across one of her bare breasts. She let her gaze linger on his long fingers, the well-shaped nails with their narrow crescent moons at the base, the fine gold-tinged skin. There was a tiny scar between his index and middle fingers, a fine line of white against the sun-bronzed flesh, and she wondered how he'd got it.

Her throat ached with unshed tears.

All the things she would never know about him. How many nights like last night would it take to have all those questions answered?

Closing her eyes, she steeled herself to inch her body away from his. It went against every instinct she possessed, but then she remembered what he had said last night.

It could be worse... You might be some spoilt little rich girl with a title and a trust fund.

She stood up unsteadily, clenching her hands into fists and pressing them to her temples as the tears spilled down her cheeks. She had no alternative but to leave. He would find out about her sooner or later, and she couldn't face the contempt in his face when he did. This might feel as if she were cutting out her own heart with a pair of nail scissors, but at least she would walk away with the memory of something perfect.

She shivered and, not trusting herself to look down on his sleeping face, gathered up the clothes they had discarded last night. She put on the shirt again, and bit her lip. If she was going to make her own way to the ferry terminal on the island she was going to need something a bit less revealing to wear.

Hesitantly she picked up his jeans. They were well-washed and soft and, although they dwarfed her slim hips, she quickly threaded the sequinned scarf through the belt loops and pulled them in to her waist, turning up the legs to mid-calf.

His mobile phone was in the back pocket. She took it out and placed it gently on top of the picnic basket where he would see it.

It was getting lighter. Soon the air would lose its haze of purple secrecy and become tinged with the soft pink of the new day. Hugging her arms around her, Anna looked out to sea, where Angelo's yacht slept serenely on the smooth water, its glass surfaces reflecting the rosy glow of the sky to the east. There was no reason for her to go back there; she had left nothing behind. Except her heart, and that didn't belong to her any more anyway.

A few metres beyond where they had slept the soft white sand gave way to the hard, smooth, tide-washed beach. Impulsively she walked towards it and, picking up a shell, bent to write a message for him. Tears splashed from her eyes and disappeared into the sand, leaving no mark.

She couldn't help herself from walking back to the rug and looking down on him. He looked young, not so very much different from that lonely boy in the orphanage, his blond hair tousled, his beautiful mouth slightly open, his dark lashes sweeping down over his cheeks.

Inhaling brokenly, she tried to stifle the sobs that tore through her and turned away to stumble blindly across the sand.

At the top of the dune she looked back, but the view was veiled behind a mist of tears.

The island was tiny and Anna knew she wouldn't have far to walk before she reached the little ferry port back to the mainland. It had been inhabited solely by the monks who had lived there since the fifth century; she felt no fear walking on her own through the shadowy forests of pine and eucalyptus in the hazy mist of the early morning.

In fact she felt nothing. She simply concentrated on putting one bare foot in front of the other, and the details of what she would do next. Arrive at Cannes. Go back to the GreenPlanet camp to pick up the few things she had left there. Take a bus to Nice. Book a flight home.

The feeling would come later.

Angelo woke with a start and sat up, instantly alert.

The beach was empty in the clear grey early morning light,

the slight indentation in the sand where she had slept beside him cold. Anna was gone.

Swiftly he pulled on his boxer shorts and looked around for the rest of his clothes. The T-shirt he had worn was lying on the sand a little way off where Anna had thrown it last night, but there was no sign of his jeans. Swearing savagely, he stood up and, seeing the writing in the sand, swore again.

THANK YOU

Gesù, she had taken his clothes and slipped away in the night, leaving a message saying *thank you*? She may as well have left a 'with compliments' slip and a mint on the pillow, the cold-hearted bitch. The shell that she had used to write in the sand was lying where she had dropped it, and beside it he noticed the prints left by her small feet.

With another muffled curse, he picked up the shell and hurled it along the beach, then stood motionless for a moment.

He had had the best night's sleep he could remember having for years. But he had broken his own golden rule and had ended up paying the price.

He had left himself vulnerable, and she had exploited that.

Bitch.

It had taken less than half an hour to reach the little ferry port, but by the time she got there Anna was exhausted with the effort of not thinking about Angelo. It had taken every ounce of will-power she had to keep her mind focused on the practical details of the day ahead, and a ruthlessness she didn't know she had to banish the images that kept flickering in front of her mind's eye like some masochistic internal slide-show. Angelo laughing, Angelo's broad bare shoulders as she'd looked down on them in the villa, Angelo sleeping.

It was that last image that was the most haunting.

Her bare feet were sore from the rough unmade island roads, bloodied where pine needles had pierced them. She didn't feel it, but when she arrived at the port and discovered that the first ferry back to the mainland didn't leave until midday, that was when she almost gave way to tears. The thought of waiting there, of Angelo coming to find her and confronting her, filled her with panic.

But the thought of waiting there and him not coming to find her was even worse.

In the end she was spared the torment. Salvation came in the form of two monks from the monastery, arriving in a battered old pick-up truck with crates of wine and honey in the back. These were the products which the monastery produced for sale, and were to be transported in their boat over to the mainland. Seeing Anna's ill-fitting clothes and tear-stained face, they agreed to take her across with them without hesitation.

'Est-ce que vous bien, ma petite?' one of them asked quietly and looking into his kindly, serene face she was filled with resolve.

'Yes,' she replied with fierce determination. 'I'm going to be fine.'

Catching the bus that went along the coast road past the château was worse. She had arrived at the same time as the first of the day's tourists, pristine in fresh summer dresses and neatly pressed shorts, and was aware of their eyes on her obviously borrowed clothes. It was a relief to disembark at the gates of the château and escape their curious glances and whispered speculation.

The GreenPlanet camp was still sleeping. Wincing at the noise, Anna unzipped the entrance to her tent. Her belongings were pretty much as she had left them, and she was relieved to see that someone had brought her things back from the beach the other night. Fliss's dress was there, folded on her rucksack in a slither of silk, alongside her little Indian bag. Rummaging in it, she found her mobile phone and squinted at the screen in the unearthly green light filtering through the canvas.

42 missed calls.

She scrolled through them. There were a couple from Fliss, but the vast majority were from the solicitors and the estate agents. She activated her voice mail and listened.

The initially impassive tone of various secretaries grew increasingly desperate, until eventually messages were being left by senior partners at the solicitors and Monsieur Ducasse himself at the estate agents. Their client was *most keen*, he stressed in his impeccable, formal English, to complete the purchase *with the utmost urgency…*

Of course he was, thought Anna dully. *He wanted to get those papers signed and the sale completed while he had me on board. No wonder he wanted to keep me another night.*

In the final message, left at about six p.m. yesterday, Monsieur Ducasse stated that the sale was in jeopardy if she didn't make contact before ten a.m. this morning. That must have been Angelo's last-ditch attempt to get things signed and sealed because he had known he would be returning her this morning.

She looked at her watch. Still only nine o'clock.

Hurriedly she rifled through her rucksack for some clean clothes, remembering with a groan that she'd left her only decent dress in Fliss's hotel room. None of the rest of her tattered and tie-dyed clothes seemed remotely suitable or appealing. *Have I changed that much in just two days?* she thought, pulling out a long tiered gypsy skirt and a midriff-skimming white cotton top. It felt like dressing up as someone else, putting on a costume to act a role in a play.

Outside the tent she could hear sleepy voices and the familiar sound of the camp waking up. With one last look around, she picked up her bag and started to walk in the direction of the road.

She hadn't gone very far when there was a shout behind her.

'Anna! Bloody hell, you're back! Where did you get to?'

'Hi, Gavin.' She smiled wearily, setting down her rucksack. 'It's a long story.'

'OK, well, let me tell you this first, then. I've found out what Emiliani has in mind for the château, and the good news is that I'm pretty sure we can stop him. He wants to turn it into a research centre for childhood respiratory diseases—asthma, tuberculosis, that sort of thing—which is why Grafton-Tarrant are on board, and we're pretty sure the plans will include some sort of residential or clinical type facility. I think that once the word *tuberculosis* gets out there our work is done...'

'No.'

'It's almost *too* easy. We won't even have to bother dredging up all the animal rights scandals attached to Grafton-Tarrant...'

'No, Gavin. I'm signing the papers. Today.'

Gavin blinked. '*What?* What about the pine forest...the landing strip...the château being stripped of its features and made into a *clinic*?'

She looked at him steadily, her new-found confidence surging through her. 'I'm sorry, Gavin. Château Belle-Eden is just a building...an empty old building with a lot of memories and ghosts, and it's probably high time it was put to some good use. A research centre for childhood respiratory diseases sounds like a wonderful idea. I'm letting it go. Sorry, I know you've worked hard.'

Gavin's small, short-sighted eyes looked peculiarly naked without his glasses. He ran a shaking hand over his matted hair.

'Why, Anna?'

She picked up her rucksack. 'Because buildings don't need protecting. People do.'

'My God.' He shook his head disbelievingly, his voice suddenly very cold. 'You've changed.'

'I know.' She smiled sadly at him. 'Goodbye, Gavin.'

Walking back towards the road, Anna took out her phone and dialled.

'Monsieur Ducasse? It's Roseanna Delafield. I'm on my way to Nice now to sign the sale contract.'

Dropping her phone back into her bag, she turned around. Behind her, above the trees, she could just make out the pinnacled tip of one turret.

'Goodbye,' she whispered, feeling a lone tear slide down her cheek.

Walking on, she dashed it away impatiently. She knew it wasn't the loss of the château she was crying for. It was the loss of Angelo.

Later that afternoon Angelo arrived at the Nice office of the Marquess of Ifford's solicitors for what should have been his moment of triumph. His PA had called mid-morning to let him know that his legal team had just had confirmation that the papers had been signed agreeing the sale of the château.

He had won.

Standing in the extremely upmarket waiting area, he wondered why he didn't feel like the victor.

This was the realization of a long-held ambition, the culmination of twelve years of private planning. He had hoped that funding a designated research centre for childhood asthma, and combining it with a state-of-the-art treatment centre for respiratory illness, would bring him just a tiny bit closer to the inner peace that had always eluded him.

He sighed, tipping his head back and gazing up at the impossibly ornate chandelier above in black despair.

It was the same old story.

Once his goal was in sight, achieving it ceased to bring him any sense of satisfaction at all. This was supposed to lay the ghost of Lucia to rest, make him feel that he had done something for her.

It didn't.

He felt colder and emptier inside than ever.

'Signor Emiliani? Monsieur Clermont will see you now.'

Angelo stood up and followed the petite blonde secretary into the solicitor's office, noticing her narrow back and long legs automatically and completely without interest.

Where was Anna now?

The thought took him by surprise, causing an odd pain somewhere in his gut. Her face swum in front of his eyes until he wondered what was the matter with him.

'Are you all right, *monsieur*?'

He looked distractedly across the desk. Monsieur Clermont's face was creased into a frown of concern and Angelo realised he hadn't heard a word that he'd said.

'Yes. Sorry, I'm just tired. It's been a difficult deal to finalise.'

Anna's mutinous face and defiant eyes flashed into his mind.

Monsieur Clermont smiled. 'I'm sorry. Lady Delafield was most apologetic when she arrived this morning to sign the papers. Hopefully now everything should proceed smoothly. Please—if you could sign in the places I've indicated…?'

'Sure.'

Angelo's eyes skimmed the document, swiftly checking and double checking the details.

He swore softly as he read the name printed on the contract again. Checked the spiky black signature.

Roseanna Josephine Delafield.

So that was the real identity of the mysterious Anna Field.

CHAPTER ELEVEN

England. One month later.

THE cold wind cut through the stable yard, sending a hail of fallen leaves scurrying across the ancient cobbles. Autumn had come early this year in a succession of cold damp days that perfectly matched Anna's mood.

It was difficult to get through them.

Locking up the dairy with stiff fingers, she sighed and leaned her head briefly against the door. She had spent the afternoon with a party of eager seven-year-olds from a local primary school, showing them how to churn butter and make bread, and the cold had seeped through the thin cotton of her Victorian dairy maid's dress into her bones, wrapping itself around the icy lump of her heart. The children's enthusiasm had been sweet and touching but, like everything else since she'd returned from France, she observed it rather than felt it.

She used to hate the days when Ifford was opened to the public, and remembered the scorn and derision with which she had regarded the steady stream of visitors who had toured the chilly staterooms and echoing marble halls with their painted ranks of scowling Delafield ancestors.

Times had changed. She had changed. She was ashamed of her former arrogance. She had thought she was so liberal, rejecting everything her family stood for, but she had just been cowardly. And in denial about her own snobbishness.

Well, Angelo would have been proud if he had seen her this afternoon. She smiled, remembering how one little girl had stroked a hand down the crisp sprigged cotton of her dress and said, 'I like your dress, miss. It's beautiful. I wish I was a dairy maid.'

Anna had knelt in front of her, and fixed her firmly in the eye. 'What's your name?'

'Emma, miss.'

'Well, Emma, I'm going to let you into a secret. If you were alive one hundred years ago, you would have considered yourself quite lucky to be a dairy maid. You would have had to get up very early in the morning—about five o'clock, in the cold with no heating and no light, and you would have had to work all day, hard, for very little money and hardly any time off. And your hands would have hurt from the cold and the damp. And choice and freedom and relaxation would have been things that you couldn't ever really hope to have, but you wouldn't worry about that because you'd be so glad to have a roof over your head and some money coming in. And you'd need the money because you would have to send it home to your mother because you've got five brothers and sisters at home who need food, and the baby's sick and the medicine she needs is expensive.'

'Why do I have to pay for it out of *my* money? That's not fair!' Emma had wailed indignantly.

Anna had paused and smiled sadly. 'Exactly.' She'd stood up, brushing a hand down her white apron. 'Life isn't fair. *Wasn't* fair. It was full of misery and exploitation. Of people forced into rigid roles and restricted and repressed.'

How easily his words came back to her. If only she could forget them.

Forget him.

'Are there any questions?' The children had stared up at her, enraptured. Then one of the boys had asked shyly, 'Are you really a real Lady?'

No.

'It's just a name,' Anna had said briskly. 'Anyone else? No, well, I think it's time for you to get your things and get back to the coach. Mrs Harris?'

The teacher had smiled at her in admiration. 'Yes, yes, thank you, Lady Delafield, it's been fascinating. Very informative, hasn't it, children?'

A chorus of enthusiastic agreement had risen from twenty-three small mouths, followed by a babble of excited chatter. Anna had shouted her goodbyes above the din and turned and left the dairy.

But, stepping out into the thin afternoon sunshine, the smile faded from her face. That was the busy part of the day finished, the part where she was saved from her own thoughts, and now the quiet hours of the late afternoon beckoned, where there was nothing to do but make dinner for her father's increasingly weak appetite and steel herself for another long, dark night.

Of course, it was the nights that were the worst.

During the interminable dark hours it was impossible to stop her thoughts from straying to Angelo. Wondering where he was and, agonisingly, who he was with. Sometimes, driven to distraction by hour upon hour of tossing and turning, worn out and defeated by the hopelessness of trying to focus her thoughts on something else, she would get up and sit on the window-seat in her bedroom and confront her fears. *He was on the yacht, he was with a beautiful blonde woman, they were laughing, drinking champagne, collapsing into bed. He was undressing her, tracing his long fingers over her perfect body...*

And then the masochistic fantasy would slip inexorably into blissful memory.

He was dancing with her on the beach at the château, he was hauling her off the pole on the yacht and throwing her on the bed, he was laying her down on the sand at St Honorat and making her weep with ecstasy...

Hugging herself in the darkness, she would look up at the serene face of the moon, hanging low over the horse chestnut trees at the edge of the parkland, and wonder if he was looking at it too. And it was in those moments that she wondered if she'd ever be happy again.

The answer seemed horrifyingly obvious.

She straightened up abruptly, pushing back the hair that was blowing across her face with a nervous flick of her hand and walking briskly towards the tack room. The really grim thing about being totally desolate, Anna had discovered, was that the world kept spinning. Days kept coming, with hours that needed to be filled with other stuff besides crying and watching black and white movies in the afternoon.

Other stuff besides dwelling on the humiliation. The sadness. On Angelo.

Grabbing a saddle and bridle, she looked down doubtfully at the ridiculous dairy maid costume for a second. She should get changed, obviously, but that would mean going back into the house and getting caught up in conversation and probably making tea for her father. An awkward peace had settled between them and she was doing her best to make amends for the years of pain she had given him, but it wasn't easy. Not when she was also carrying around the heavy burden of her broken heart.

She couldn't face it.

Speaking soothingly, softly, she unbolted the stable door of her father's chestnut hunter. Since she'd been back she'd taken to riding him round the parkland often, and the exercise was beginning to tell in the improved condition of his glossy coat. He tossed his head as she slid the saddle swiftly on to his back, eager to be off.

It wasn't until she had led him out into the stable yard that she realised she hadn't got her hard hat.

So what? she thought despairingly, springing into the saddle in a billow of skirts. My heart's already in pieces. I'm not sure that anything much worse could happen.

Setting her chin determinedly, she kicked the horse on and clattered out of the yard.

Angelo brought the helicopter in lower, letting his gaze drift over the picture-perfect patchwork of fields and hedges below him. There was something peculiarly beautiful about autumn in England. This was Anna's landscape, he thought grimly—peculiarly magnificent, but somehow sad. The trees wore their autumn colours with great bravado, but already one could see the bare branches beneath the red and gold—naked, vulnerable, just like Anna.

The thought needled him and his knuckles were white on the gear lever as he circled and banked, looking for the house. Whether she was sad or happy or bloody over-the-moon was of absolutely no interest to him whatsoever, he reminded himself tersely. He was only here on a completely practical matter.

That was all.

The last month had been non-stop and he'd hardly had time to draw breath, never mind dwell on Anna. He had two more projects on the go—exciting ones, in Corsica and Ibiza. Of course he was too busy to wonder how she was and what she was doing. He probably would have forgotten her altogether had it not been for a call from the building manager on site at the château, asking him what to do with all the stuff in the attic.

His automatic response had been, 'Dispose of it.' Ending the call curtly, he had tried to get back to the other business of his meeting with the financial team, but had found it impossible to concentrate on profit margin and potential growth. Excusing himself abruptly, he had left the meeting and phoned back.

'What is there in the attic?'

'Nothing of value. You're right, *signor*, it should be disposed of. I'll see to—'

'I asked what there is.'

'A few boxes. Photographs and letters. Some kids' stuff—dressing-up clothes and a dolls' house.'

'Keep it.'

'*Signor?*'

'I said keep it. I'll be down later.'

Late that evening, after a day in the Rome office, he'd flown the helicopter back to the château and gone up to the attic. The light had been fading, casting hazy rainbows on the majestic staircase as he'd run up it, two steps at a time, trying not to think of her as he had first seen her there.

He'd seen the dress straight away, draped over an old wash-stand as if she had taken it off and dropped it there only minutes ago. Picking it up, he'd held it out in front of him.

A miniature wedding dress.

Ragged. Mildewed. Fit only for disposal.

The sharp noise of self-disgust he made now was drowned out by the noise of the helicopter. It wasn't his to throw away, he rationalized impatiently, which was why it was currently in the back, wrapped in tissue paper and folded carefully into a box.

Below him he could see the rolling parkland and lush woodland of Ifford Park and the sight sent a shot of adrenalin-fuelled indignation through his veins that made him bring the helicopter into a steep upwards climb. The sulky, vulnerable, sensitive girl he was remembering from the yacht was an act. That was Anna Field, and she didn't exist.

The person he was about to meet was Lady Roseanna Delafield. Heiress, aristo-party girl, deceiving bitch.

It would be good to confront her with some of that.

Swooping low over the trees, he looked for somewhere suitable to land. To the right he could see the imposing house, with its stone frontage and pillared portico, its outbuildings arranged around a courtyard to one side. The wide sweep of lawn to the front of the house was flanked by huge sycamore trees, making it impossible to land there, so he banked away again, going out and beyond the trees to more open ground, and coming down lower again.

As he did so he noticed a dark shape break from the cover of the trees, moving at breakneck speed into the open. Cursing violently in Italian, he saw that it was a horse and rider and swung the helicopter almost vertically back into the sky.

Righting it again, he swung round in a circle, banking around the fixed point of the house, frantically scanning the ground below for any sign of them. On the controls his hands were perfectly steady but his jaw was set in a tight line of tension, which softened slightly as he spotted the horse for a moment as it galloped beneath the trees some distance away. It was another split second before he realised with a sickening lurch of his stomach that the rider was no longer astride.

With ice-cold precision he brought the helicopter in to land and, without waiting for the blades to stop spinning, leapt down, running across the uneven grass to the horribly still figure on the ground. As he grew nearer he felt the colour drain from his face and the acid rise to his throat.

No. God, no. Please don't let it be—

He knelt on the damp grass and reached out a shaking hand to the slender neck beneath the tumble of dark hair, with its fading streaks of pink.

It was Anna.

But the faint flutter of a pulse told him she was alive.

Thank God.

CHAPTER TWELVE

ANGELO pressed his fists to his temples in a despairing attempt to stop himself from snatching Anna up and pressing her to him. Somewhere in the recesses of his frozen brain he was still thinking rationally enough to know that he mustn't move her in case her spine was damaged.

Why, *per l'amore di dio*, hadn't she been wearing a hard hat?

Ruthlessly suppressing the panic that was swelling inside him, he moved around to the other side of her, so he could see her face.

He gritted his teeth and forced himself to stand back, not to touch her. Dark lashes swept over cheeks that were deathly pale but, other than that, her face was exactly…the same. The same face that had drifted in and out of his broken dreams and restless nights for the last month.

He let out a desolate moan and sank to his knees beside her, feeling in the pocket of his jacket for his mobile and jabbing the emergency service number with shaking fingers.

'Wh—what—?'

Her eyes opened just a crack, but enough for her to see the face that swam hazily in front of her like some fierce guardian angel. It looked like Angelo's face, but it couldn't be, because Angelo was in Italy—or was it France?—and he was making love to beautiful blonde women and, anyway, his eyes were cold, cold, cold, and these eyes burned with…

'*No!*'

Anna struggled to sit up. She knew what this meant. When you saw angels and felt surrounded by love—that meant you were dying. And she wasn't ready to die now.

'*No! no!*'

Strong arms went round her, a hard body covered her own, easing her gently back on to the ground, cushioning her, cradling her with infinite tenderness. And it was Angelo's voice she heard, murmuring, Angelo's scent that filled her nostrils, Angelo's warmth against her cold cheek.

Oh, please…yes…don't make this stop. If this is death, I'll take it…

She felt the tears squeeze from beneath her closed eyelids as she stopped fighting and surrendered, going limp and pliant in his arms.

'Anna. *Gesù—Anna?*'

His hands cupped her face and then, miraculously, his lips brushed against hers. With a moan of longing, she tilted her face upwards and caught his mouth with hers, kissing him hungrily, with all the pent-up despair and hopeless longing of the past empty month. Helplessly she felt her arms snake around his neck until she was clinging to him, kissing the life out of him. Kissing the life back into herself.

'Anna, stop!' His voice was like ground glass. 'You might be hurt.'

He disentangled himself, holding her away from him at arm's length so he could look into her face. Apart from the pallor and two faint crescents of blue beneath her eyes she looked OK, but he couldn't take any chances.

'I need to call an ambulance. Please, until they get here, lie still.'

'What are you doing here?'

He tried to keep his tone light, not let her see the panic that was pulsing through his veins. 'I came to see you, which under the circumstances was just as well. What the hell do you think you're playing at, riding like a madwoman, without a hat? You could have been killed.'

'Only because of you,' she said faintly. 'It was the helicopter that scared the horse.' She sank back on to the grass, waiting for the pounding in her head to subside. It didn't.

'*Dio*, Anna, I didn't come here to argue with you,' he muttered through gritted teeth. 'I think we both had enough of that last time. Just do as you're told for once in your life and lie still, please.'

'I'm fine.' Suddenly she realized that the top of her ridiculously low-cut and inauthentic dairy maid costume had slipped down off one shoulder and her breasts were spilling over the top. Ineffectually she tugged at it, grateful that at least she still had the vestiges of her Riviera tan. She giggled weakly. She could hardly be at death's door if all she could think about was her cleavage.

She struggled into an upright position and began to tentatively flex her arms and legs. 'Look. No damage done.' She frowned up at him as the darkness seemed to gather behind his blond head, concentrating the light around him like a halo. She felt suddenly very, very tired.

'Angelo, you are here, aren't you? I haven't imagined you, have I? Am I going to wake up and find this is just another wonderful, cruel dream? Because, if I do, I can't bear it, I—'

He just managed to catch her as she blacked out.

'Concussion.'

Angelo stood up as the doctor came into the sitting room. He'd been trying to make a fire out of the meagre amount of damp kindling and logs and had finally achieved a small but promising blaze. However, the temperature still felt lower in there than it was outside.

'It's nothing too serious,' the young doctor continued, 'but I want you to keep a close eye on her for the next twenty-four hours. If she shows any sign of losing consciousness again, or she's sick or confused or you're at all worried, please don't hesitate to call, Mr er…'

'I'm worried now,' Angelo growled, ignoring the courtesy. 'I think she should go to hospital.'

Dr Adams adjusted his glasses nervously. 'I can assure you, they won't be able to do anything more for her than let her rest, which she can do better here. I can understand your concern— she's had a nasty fall, but she's really been very lucky. There's absolutely no sign of any internal bleed—I've checked her over very thoroughly.'

Angelo's eyes narrowed dangerously. That was an image he didn't want to dwell on.

'She's pretty sleepy now, but make sure you wake her every hour or so, just to check she's all right. While I'm here I'll pop in on Sir William, make sure he's doing OK and fill him in on the situation, if that's all right with you?'

Angelo nodded curtly, turning towards the fire and stretching out his cold hands to the weak flames.

The doctor opened the door and was just about to leave, but hesitated and looked back at the imposing blond stranger. He was intimidatingly good-looking and exuded power and wealth, but there was something touching about the anxiety in his narrow blue eyes.

'She'll be fine, you know,' he said.

Walking down the gloomy corridor towards the library where he knew Sir William would be found, Dr Adams allowed himself a rueful smile. Whoever this guy was, he was obviously utterly besotted with Roseanna Delafield, but he'd have his hands full with her.

Lucky, lucky bloke.

Angelo knocked gently on the heavy oak door to Anna's room and, hearing no sound, pushed it open.

Madre di dio, it was even colder up here. That was why he was shivering so violently.

Lying in the enormous four-poster bed with its dark red curtains of moth-eaten velvet, Anna looked about twelve years old. Angelo felt his heart miss a beat at the sight of her porcelain-pale face, her dark hair falling back on to the pillow. For a moment he gazed helplessly down on her. Since the summer the pink had begun to grow out of her hair and she'd lost weight, so that her face had a new angularity. She had lost some of that childlike softness he remembered and, devouring her with his eyes, he noticed her arms were thinner. Stifling a groan of physical pain, he remembered the sinuous grace with which she'd swung around the pole on the yacht. God, she didn't look strong enough to lift a spoon now.

His throat tightened and he felt as if a lead weight were crushing his chest. The hour that had passed since he had carried her in here after the fall felt like a week. She'd drifted back to consciousness pretty quickly, but had been drowsy and confused, and he had had to hold her against his chest as he'd undone the little hooks at the back of the odd Victorian-style dress she was wearing. At one point her head had rolled sideways, off his shoulder, and he had caught her, cradling her cheek against his hand, finding himself unable to stop shaking as he'd felt her fragility.

That was the point when he'd found himself right up against the wall, facing the black shadow of his own private nemesis. There was nowhere else to run. He had nothing with which to defend himself against the emotion which rampaged through him.

Easing the bodice down off her shoulders, he had lain her down on the bed and searched around for something in which to dress her. Reaching under the pillows, he had grasped what he'd assumed was her nightdress and pulled it out.

It was his shirt—the one he had put on her in the Villa Santa Domitilla.

He pulled a ridiculously low, threadbare chair over to Anna's bedside and settled himself into it. Up until now he had automatically dealt with emotion by ruthlessly blanking it out—by distracting himself with the next project, the next hand of cards, the next blonde. He'd thought that by now his heart had simply shrivelled and died.

Discovering that it hadn't, that in fact he was as susceptible, as fallible, as capable of falling headlong in love with someone should have come as a huge relief. *Would* have done. If only it hadn't been so bloody excruciatingly painful.

For numberless hours he sat beside her, watching her face as the afternoon shadows deepened and he couldn't see her properly any more. Not that it mattered. Every curve of lip and cheekbone, every eyelash was imprinted on his mind like a photograph.

But it was cold. Like the cold of the orphanage, he thought bleakly, getting up and stretching his cramped limbs. And to think he had scathingly condemned her for her privileged upbringing. This place was straight out of Dickens.

'Anna?' He shook her gently, using every ounce of self-control he possessed to keep his hand on her shoulder and not slide it into the thick tangle of her hair. She moved her head slightly, but didn't open her eyes. He bent down to her, feeling the whisper of her breath against his cheek and pressed his lips to her forehead.

'Anna, *dolce amore*, open your eyes for me, please.'

She murmured and stirred, her dark lashes fluttering like the wings of some exotic butterfly against her blue-shadowed skin. Beneath them he caught the glint of her dark eyes and felt his breathing steady again. She was all right.

'I'm going to make you a cup of tea.'

A frown creased her smooth forehead and she lifted a hand to her temple. Angelo took it in his, trying to keep the anguish from showing on his face as he felt the bones beneath the skin.

'Go back to sleep.'

'But...my father. I have to...'

'Don't worry about anything. Leave it to me.' He was aware that his voice sounded harsh and cold, but was terrified of letting her see how scared he was.

How raw.

She turned her head away from him as a tear trickled down her cheek and into her hair. 'I'm sorry, Angelo.'

He sighed. 'Don't be silly. Now, tell me where to find your father and go back to sleep.'

'Library.'

'Good girl.' He crossed the room, fists clenched, wondering if she was thinking, as he was, of that night on the beach when he had teased her with those words, but, glancing back at the bed, she seemed to have drifted back into sleep.

'Sir William?'

The old man was sitting in the evening gloom, staring out of the window, the embers of a dead fire glowing feebly in the grate, but he looked up when Angelo entered the room. Striding across to where he sat, Angelo extended a hand. 'I'm Angelo Emiliani. Please don't stand.'

Sir William sank back into his chair gratefully. His hand was thin but surprisingly strong and the eyes that met Angelo's were sharp.

'So you're the chap who bought the château. Hope you didn't come here to tell me you want your money back. Too late, I'm afraid—all gone to the blasted taxman already. Have you seen Rose?'

For a moment Angelo was confused. 'Rose?'

'Yes. Doctor said she'd had a fall.'

'Oh, Anna! She's asleep.'

Sir William laughed wheezily. 'Ever the chameleon. D'you know, one summer she kept two boyfriends on the go by pretending she had a sister. So one of them always asked for Rose and the other one for Anna. One was terribly respectable, took her to the ballet and all that carry-on, while the other was a tearaway with a motorbike.' He shook his head. 'I could never keep up with her.'

Angelo smiled bleakly. 'I'm afraid that makes two of us.'

The old man's face looked suddenly sad. 'Lisette understood her. Damn tragedy that she died. For Roseanna and for me.' He looked up at the portrait of an incredibly beautiful blonde woman which was over the fireplace. She was dressed in a clinging scarlet evening dress; the painter had captured exactly the glow of her golden skin, so that in the darkling gloom of the dank room it seemed to give out light. Angelo thrust his hands in his pockets and looked up at the picture. Something bothered him about it.

'Anna's mother?'

She wasn't at all like Anna. Ice-cool, elegant, her beauty had a look-but-don't-touch air that made him shiver. Anna's heat and vitality seemed suddenly even braver and more special by comparison.

'Anyway, you didn't come here to hear ancient family history. What can I do for you?'

'I came to return some things that got left behind in the château. In the attics there were some photos and letters and clothes.'

Sir William snorted. 'Jolly decent of you, but you could have saved yourself the trouble. Nothing there that I want. Never liked the place. Avoided it.' He looked suddenly agitated. 'Letters, you say? Photographs? Best just get rid of it all. Don't want to rake over old wounds now.'

'Of course,' Angelo replied with impeccable courtesy. There was something odd about the other man's reaction. 'Do you think Anna would like to keep any of it, if it belonged to her mother…?'

Sir William's head jerked upwards, his eyes blazing. '*No!* I don't want you showing any of it to her, d'you hear me? It's private. Personal. It all happened a long time ago. She's been upset enough—finding out about all that would just hurt her more.'

'Finding out about what?'

For a moment Angelo thought the old man hadn't heard him, or had chosen not to answer, but then he spoke. 'The baby. Lisette…' His voice was harsh with remembered pain. 'It was the summer we got engaged. She was too young, really—too young by far for an old bachelor like me, but her parents wanted it. The title, you see? Anyway, that summer she went back to Belle-Eden to plan the wedding and met some chap.' He gave a short, bitter laugh. 'Of course her parents were having none of it. Forbade her to see him. But the damage was already done, d'you see?'

Angelo looked up at the golden girl in the picture. 'She got pregnant?'

Sir William gave an almost imperceptible nod. 'But Roseanna doesn't know. When Lisette was alive she was too young to understand, and now… Well, it could only make things worse. She mustn't see those letters, d'you understand?'

Angelo saw the old man's distress and felt a twinge of pity. 'I understand. Now, if you'll excuse me, I came to make a cup of tea for Anna. Could I bring one for you too?'

'What?' The old man was lost in a world of his own. 'Oh, yes. Yes. Kitchen's across the hall and along the passage to the left. Bit of a mess, I'm afraid. Mrs Haskett's in again tomorrow.'

Reaching the door, Angelo paused and turned back. 'If you don't mind me asking, what happened to the baby?'

Sir William looked at him vaguely, as if struggling to remember. 'Hmm? The baby? Adopted, I suppose.'

Angelo nodded thoughtfully and opened the door. Instantly the draught from the passageway outside curled around him like the caress of a ghost and followed him along the dim hallway towards the kitchen.

'Bit of a mess' had been something of an understatement. Washing-up was piled in the sink and assorted cats lay about on surfaces and along the length of the huge scrubbed pine table in the centre of the room. Putting the large kettle on to the hotplate of an old, chipped Aga, Angelo found himself fighting the temptation to go upstairs, gather Anna up in his arms and fly her somewhere where he could make her warm and comfortable and take care of her properly.

Leaning against the rail of the Aga while he waited for the kettle to boil, he dropped his head briefly into his hands in an agony of despair and frustration. The reality was that he could do nothing. He was utterly powerless. The feeling was as unpleasant as it was unfamiliar.

He rubbed his cold fingers over his forehead and thought about the conversation he'd just had with Anna's father.

Adopted, I suppose... He had made it sound so insignificant, and Angelo felt his lip curl into a sneer of contempt.

To his sort it probably was. It only reinforced what Angelo had suspected about the aristocracy all along. A baby with a blemished bloodline was worth nothing.

Clumsily, feeling dizzy and disorientated, Anna made her way slowly down the stairs. Dr Adams had given her something to take the edge off the pain in her head and the gathering ache in her shoulders and ribs, but it had also made everything else feel slightly fuzzy.

Like the fact that Angelo Emiliani was downstairs in the kitchen making tea.

The image was so unlikely that she wondered if she'd dreamt it. Maybe the fall had made her hallucinate? Which would also mean she'd imagined the bit where he'd carried her upstairs and held her against him as he'd taken off her dress. She felt the blood flood into her cheeks as she remembered how he had pulled back the cover on her bed and looked beneath her pillow for a nightdress, eventually unearthing the garment she'd been sleeping in since she'd left him in St Honorat.

His shirt.

Pausing to steady herself against the wall of the kitchen passageway, she bit her lip. Oh, God, how deeply, desperately embarrassing. Nothing could have made her feelings more obvious really, which he would either find amusing or just tedious and awkward. She took a deep breath and walked down the passageway to the kitchen, stopping in the doorway. He was standing against the Aga, his head in his hands in an attitude of utter despair.

An icy chill crept into her heart. So that answered that, then.

Glancing around the kitchen she could suddenly see it as he must see it. Compared to the sleek perfection of the yacht, this must seem like the armpit of the universe.

She was about to flee back upstairs when he looked up.

'Anna, you shouldn't be out of bed. I'm bringing you some tea.'

'I'm fine, honestly,' she said, doing her best impression of bright and cheerful. 'I'll make the tea. I should take some in to my father. He'll be wondering what's happened to me.'

'It's all in hand. Stop worrying.'

She spun round. 'You've seen my father?'

'Yes, and I found the number for Mrs Haskett and I've arranged for her to come down first thing tomorrow—and bring some groceries.' His voice was harsh and impatient, filling her with black despair. Perhaps he noticed that because, with a heroic effort, he softened it and said, 'Really, there's nothing for you to worry about.'

Yeah, right. The tidying up was in hand. Shopping was being delivered. That would just leave the embarrassing detail that she was head-over-heels in love with him, then.

Awkwardly she nodded and looked down. 'Thanks,' she whispered. 'It's all such a mess.'

She heard him expel a heavy breath, then felt the delicious warmth and strength of his hands on her shoulders. 'Go back to bed. I'll bring the tea. And is there anything to eat in this place, apart from cat food?'

Anna reddened. 'I've been so busy with the schools, I haven't really had the time to shop.' Or the inclination. She'd lost all interest in food since she'd been back, which was possibly one of the up sides of unrequited love. She'd lived mainly on breakfast cereal and the awful instant soups favoured by her father. The langoustines and olives of St Honorat seemed to belong in another lifetime.

'Schools? Am I right in thinking that would explain your rather unusual outfit this afternoon?'

She nodded, then was struck by a thought. 'The bread! We made bread—and butter! It's out in the dairy—I'll just go and get it.'

'No! You'll go back to bed. *I'll* go and get it and if you're not in bed when I come up there'll be trouble.'

Going back upstairs, Anna's heart felt like lead in her chest.

He was here and he was being so wonderful. This was everything she'd dreamed of, so why wasn't she swinging from the chandeliers with joy?

Because she had trapped him. He felt guilty, obviously, for the accident, and he couldn't leave until he was sure she was OK. The doctor had probably even told him as much, so he was stuck here until she was deemed to be well enough to leave on her own. Twenty-four hours?

Twenty-four hours.

It wasn't much, but it was all she had to keep her going—maybe for a lifetime.

He was back in twenty minutes, balancing a tray on one hand as he kicked the door to her room shut to keep out the draught that curled through the passages of the old house.

Sitting up in bed, Anna smiled bravely. No tears, no neediness, but as she watched him walk towards her she felt her heart give a painful kick.

The late September light was failing outside and the sky in the west over the parkland was streaked with fire. In the gloom and shabbiness of the room he seemed more golden and perfect than ever. In some strange way he suddenly reminded her of her mother. Maybe it was his beauty. Maybe it was the fact that, for however briefly, he was looking after her.

'So,' he said gravely, setting the tray down on the end of the bed and coming to sit beside her, 'I have to admit that you're the first pole-dancing, aristocratic eco-warrior I've ever met who can also bake a great loaf of bread. You're full of surprises, Lady Delafield.'

Anna grinned weakly. 'I try. I'd hate to be the same as all the other pole-dancing, aristocratic eco-warriors out there.'

He laughed briefly. *Oh, God*, Anna thought, *he's bored out of his brain, he can't wait to get away.*

'I found some soup. God knows what it'll taste like, but I want you to eat something. You've got far too thin.' He held up a spoon to her lips and she parted them, looking into his eyes.

The room fell silent, apart from the hammering of her heart. It was so dark now that it was impossible to make out the expression on his face.

'Why didn't you tell me who you were, when we were on the yacht?' he asked, tearing off a mouthful of bread with those long poetic fingers and offering it to her.

She leaned back on the pillows, sighing softly.

'Do you remember you accused me of making assumptions?'

He nodded, his face in shadow.

'Well, you were right. I did do that. But I think that's because I've had a lifetime of people doing it to me. Lady Roseanna Delafield—daughter of a Marquess. Spoiled, rich, brought up in the lap of luxury with an army of servants. That's what people always assume. And, as you've seen, that's not how it is.' She hesitated and bit her lip, struggling to find the words to confront her old demon. Her secret shame.

'No,' he said dryly. 'Go on.'

'It's also not who I am. I don't belong here. I found—' She faltered. She could see his profile silhouetted against the window. He was so unreachable, so remote, and all of a sudden she was reminded of that lonely boy in the orphanage. The words died on her lips. She would not start whining about her own sense of isolation and lack of identity. Not to this man who had had none of the blessings she had been given—parents who had loved her and had been willing to look after her as their own.

'I don't know,' she finished lamely. 'I guess I've never been someone who wanted to be labelled. I've spent my life trying to avoid that.'

'Running away?'

There was a small pause as Anna digested his words.

'Maybe. Running away sometimes, but also hiding. Behind different roles. Rebel. Disciplined dancer. Activist. All of them designed to distract people from the simple fact that, underneath, I don't know who I am, and that I'm ashamed of that.'

That was the nearest she was going to get to saying it. Their eyes locked and she looked at him imploringly, silently willing him to understand.

'Don't be.'

Electricity seemed to be buzzing and crackling through her veins and the throbbing in her head had been drowned out by the more persistent drum-beat of the pulse between her thighs. She was trembling, so that as Angelo held the spoon to her lips again it clattered against her teeth.

Two fat tears slid down her bruised cheeks.

Turning away, he replaced the spoon in the bowl, then slowly, slowly brought his face back round to look into hers. Reaching out one hand, he cupped her jaw, brushing away the tears with his thumb. His chest felt it might implode with the effort it was taking not to crush her mouth with his and rip that bloody shirt off her. Again.

Mustering every shred of self-control he possessed, he slid an arm around her heaving shoulders and cradled her against his chest, where her hot tears soaked through his shirt.

Gradually her sobs subsided under the soothing stroke of his hand and the murmur of his lips against her hair. He didn't know how long he held her like that, but the moon had risen above the trees by the time her breathing steadied and deepened and he felt her grow heavy in his arms. He lay staring into the silvery dark, testing out his new-found emotional depth.

Not since Lucia had he allowed himself to get this close to someone without ravishing them. For him, closeness had involved nothing more than considerate foreplay, but here he was, holding this girl, kissing her hair.

He pressed a final kiss against her head, settled her more comfortably against him and lay back on the pillows.

Slipping into sleep, he felt a tiny flicker of hope glowing in the ashes of his heart.

'Angelo?'

His eyes snapped open. It was still dark, he realised, struggling into a sitting position and rubbing a hand over his face. It must be the middle of the night.

'I'm here. What is it? Are you all right?' his voice was harsh with anxiety. He'd dreamed of Lucia and had awoken with that old familiar feeling of panic.

'I'm fine. It's OK…' He felt her slim arms slip around his waist, her cheek come to rest on his back so that he could feel the warmth of her breath through his thin shirt. Then she moved so that she was kneeling in front of him. Her eyes were like liquid in the darkness, then the lashes swept down over their rich gleam.

'You were talking,' she said softly. 'About Lucia.'

He sighed and swore quietly. 'Sorry. It's a dream I have often.'

'I know what you said on the yacht, that you never sleep with…anyone…and I thought that may be why and…I didn't want to trap you into something you didn't want to…' She took a deep breath. 'I just wanted you to know that you can sleep in a guest room, if you want.'

'Do you want me to?'

For a moment he could neither see nor hear anything in the velvet blackness. Then he felt the blissful softness of her mouth on his, felt her shake her head.

'But please, if you're staying, would you get undressed?'

Her hands were already undoing the buttons of his shirt. He caught them in his, held them.

'I can't, Anna. You've got concussion, for God's sake, and I'm not such a cold-blooded bastard that I'm going to make love to you tonight.'

She sighed and pulled him down beside her, flipping on to her back. In the dull light he could just make out the outline of her breasts. His body thrummed and pulsed with raw desire.

It was a baptism of fire. Every nerve screamed to touch her, but he lay still.

His life for the last twelve years had been about instant gratification—in business and in pleasure, about taking and not keeping. But, as the cold grey light of morning filtered through the grimy window, he allowed himself a small smile of triumph. For the first time in his life he had managed to hold out. He had felt the need, experienced the longing, and resisted it.

That, he thought, was love.

CHAPTER THIRTEEN

WHEN Angelo opened his eyes again it was properly light and the bed beside him was cold and empty. This time he felt no panic but lay on his back, his hands behind his head, staring up at the faded velvet canopy over the bed. He had slept deeply and, judging by the bright, cold light falling through the grimy window, for a long time.

And he had awoken feeling at peace with himself. Today, for the first time ever that he could remember, his head was not immediately full of targets and imperatives for the day ahead. There was no buzzy need to achieve something, to score the first business advantage of the day, to better an adversary or get ahead on a deal driving him to get out of bed.

In fact, if Anna was feeling better, absolutely nothing was going to drive him out of bed today.

Right on cue the door opened and she appeared.

He felt his body harden, the jeans he had slept in, like armour, tighten. *Gesù*, he thought wryly. This was another stage of youth he'd missed out on. From the moment he'd lost his virginity at the age of sixteen to the bored thirty-something wife of a shipping magnate, he'd screwed women artfully, effortlessly, emotionlessly. But this, this heart-flipping arousal, was something he'd never experienced before.

She was wearing jeans and an enormous, thick polo-neck

sweater that highlighted the delicacy of her face and in her hands she carried two steaming mugs of coffee.

'Is it sacrilege to offer instant coffee to an Italian?'

'I suspect you could get away with offering ice cream to an Eskimo,' he said dryly, accepting one of the mugs and shifting over on the bed so she could sit down beside him. 'How are you feeling this morning?'

She smiled wickedly into his eyes, but there was a hint of uncertainty there. A question. 'Frustrated.'

He took a sip of the watery coffee, relying on the caffeine rush to counteract the far more powerful testosterone hit her words had just initiated. 'Anna, I'm being serious. How's your head?'

She reached out and took the mug from his hand, putting it on to the dusty bedside table, then swung one leg over him.

'My head's OK,' she said slowly. 'However…' she took one of his hands and slid it under her sweater '…I'm a bit concerned about my heart, doctor.'

Angelo sucked in a sharp breath as his hand encountered the soft warmth of her bare breast. He could feel her heart, beating fast beneath his palm. Slowly he sat upright and tipped her off his chest so that she was lying on the bed beside him. Carefully keeping his face perfectly blank, he pulled the curtains on one side of the bed closed in a shower of dust.

'In that case, I'd better examine you. Take your clothes off, please.'

On the bed, Anna writhed out of her jeans as Angelo viciously tugged the curtains at the end of the bed closed. In the sudden shadowy darkness she saw his throat move as he swallowed. She sat up, raising her arms to pull the sweater over her head, and as the soft wool enveloped her face she felt his hands on her ribs, sliding upwards, along her arms, easing her out of the tangle of her clothes.

'You're beautiful.'

Her hair crackled with static, but that was nothing to the

passion that snapped and fizzed in her dark, dark eyes. His gaze travelled downwards and he forced himself to go slowly, taking her in, inch by inch: the delicate outline of her collar-bone above the luscious breasts that he knew just fitted perfectly into his hands. The narrowness of her ribs, the decadent sparkle of the jewelled bar in her midriff, the pale line on her flawless skin that showed where her bikini had been…

He made a low guttural sound, caught between wanting that moment to last for ever and the need to have her, to be inside her right now, to possess her and never let her go.

She stood up on the bed and, reaching round him, unhooked the curtains on the last side of the four poster, pulling them together to enclose them in secret darkness. He could see nothing, could only feel her hands on his waist, unfastening the button on his jeans, gently working them down over his hips. He let his head fall backwards as her fingers swept across the skin beneath the top of his boxer shorts, easing them over the hard jut of his painful arousal.

He was lost, throbbing with longing. Feeling every touch as if for the first time.

Aching.

Anna let her palms linger on the hard flatness of his stomach, adoring the way she could feel his flesh quiver as her hands inched downwards. Sitting on the edge of the bed, she leaned her forehead against his chest, knowing that her mouth was only inches from his straining erection, exhaling heavily so that her breath caressed his skin. The darkness wreathed them completely, but her mind was full of images of him. She jumped as she felt his fingertips on her shoulders, then relaxed against him as they began to move in caressing, languid circles down her back.

There was no hurry, no sense of urgency in their dark paradise. Every move, every touch was filled with the pleasure of the moment. Gently he pushed her back on to the bed, leaning over her to bring his mouth down to hers and plundering it softly, lovingly before moving downwards to her neck, her breast. Only as his lips brushed her dew-drenched thigh did she cry out, at last driven to the very edges of self-control and she felt him pull away from her.

'Angelo, please...'

'Wait,' he rasped, stooping swiftly to where he'd kicked his jeans and fumbling in the pockets for a condom. 'Damn.'

'I don't care. Please...'

Her hands gripped his hips, pulling him down on to her, and the next moment a deep shudder of total surrender ricocheted through him as he felt her fingers close around the very core of his desire, guiding him into her. And then she was wrapping her slender legs around him and arching her pelvis up to take all of him inside her, and the past, the future and everything was obliterated in the pure perfection of *now*.

She was in his arms, underneath him, beside him, her hair on his face, her lips on his skin, her dark, delicious scent all around him. He was lost, but he was also home. The bliss stretched and quivered until convulsively he grasped her closer, cupping her bottom and driving deeply into her as desire spilled over into fulfilment. At the moment of his own explosion into ecstasy her soft, high gasp in his ear was like a gift.

Afterwards they lay locked together and he thought about the consequences and implications of what he'd just done. Never before, *ever*, had he had sex without protection. To him it was automatic—part of the ritual, to guard himself against disease and paternity, and maybe just to guard himself against closeness. Anna had removed that barrier as she had removed so many of the others he had built between himself and the rest of the world.

She shifted a little in his arms and he twitched the curtain aside so that a thin shaft of sunlight penetrated their warm cave.

'No-o-o!' She rolled over and buried her face in his chest. 'Too bright!'

'I want to see you.' He frowned and stroked the hair back from her face. 'Are you all right—does your head hurt?'

'No, thank you, doctor.' She smiled teasingly up at him. 'But I'm suddenly hugely hungry.'

'Is Mrs Haskett downstairs? Did she bring groceries?'

Anna moaned. 'I can't believe you can even mention the word "groceries" at a moment like this. Angelo Emiliani, there is no romance in your soul whatsoever.' Scrambling up on to her knees, he was treated to the glorious sight of her naked body as she reached up to the carved wooden headboard of the bed.

'What are you doing? Not that I'm not enjoying the view, whatever it is…'

'Aha…' She flopped down beside him again with a look of pure triumph and produced a packet of biscuits.

'Where did those come from?' He looked at her suspiciously. 'And how old are they? Anna, have those been there since you had your last sleepover party when you were about fifteen?'

'I never had sleepover parties. You're my first one.'

'Are you having a nice time?'

'Yep.' Her face was alight with happiness and it seemed to warm him from the inside, melting the ice that had slowed the passage of blood through his veins for the last eternity.

'So where did the biscuits come from?'

'Secret cupboard. Look.' She kneeled up again and he watched as she slid across one of the carved panels in the headboard. 'This is a Victorian reproduction, but during the sixteenth century Catholics used to hide their bibles and rosary beads in them.'

He quirked an eyebrow at her. 'Interesting. Do you bring parties of schoolchildren on educational visits in here too?'

'Only the very good-looking sixth-formers from the boys' school.'

'I'm sure they learn a lot,' he said dryly. 'So what do you keep in your secret cupboard, apart from biscuits?'

She shrugged, suddenly shy. 'Special things.' Taking down a small box, she shut the little cupboard again and settled herself back on the pillows, the box on her knee. 'There's the first merit award I won for ballet, and the programme from *The Nutcracker*, which my mother took me to see at Covent Garden.' She laid them out on the bed and, leaning on one elbow, he watched her face as she looked into the little box. 'That used to be lavender from the garden of the château, but look, it's shed all its flowers.' She held out the box, tipping it so that the dead flower-heads fell into her hand, along with a couple of other things.

Glancing into the palm of her hand just before her fingers closed, Angelo felt his heart stop for a second, then begin again, pumping ice through his veins.

Benedetto Gesù, it couldn't be…Please, God, let his eyes and his mind be playing tricks on him…

'What have you got there?' His throat suddenly felt as if it were made of sandpaper.

'Ah—the most precious thing of all.' Smiling softly, she uncurled her fingers. There, cupped in her hand beside the shell he had given her on St Honorat, was a ruby and diamond earring. The exact match to the one that had been tucked into the shawl he had been wrapped in when he had been found by the nuns.

'It's an incredibly rare, incredibly valuable piece,' she was saying teasingly, 'traditionally given by emotionally inarticulate Italian males to their women and meaning *I love you*…'

'I'm not talking about the shell. I mean the earring.'

To his own ears his voice sounded hollow and very far away, but if she noticed she gave nothing away.

'Oh, that. It's not an earring, it's a pendant.'

Relief flooded through him.

'Although…' Anna was holding it between her fingers, looking at the back '…oddly enough, it was an earring once, but the other one was lost so my mother had it made into a pendant for me. She inherited them from her grandmother and there was big trouble when the other one went missing. It's worth a lot, I know that much.'

Cartier. 1922.

'This, however,' Anna continued, stroking a finger over the pearly pink surface of the shell, '*this* is actually priceless…'

Angelo stood up, waiting for the nausea to subside and the fog to clear from his head, then strode across to the door. He didn't know where he was going, just that he had to put some distance between himself and Anna. There was a burning feeling in his chest.

'Angelo?'

Her voice was full of fear and it felt like tiny barbs in his heart. Gritting his teeth, he forced himself to turn back towards her, but, not trusting himself to speak, he simply looked at her, desperately trying to keep his expression blank.

'What's wrong?'

He shook his head, then left the room, closing the door very quietly behind him.

The plumbing at Ifford was as Dickensian as the rest of the God-forsaken place, thought Angelo savagely, towelling himself with a scrap of fabric that felt like sandpaper. But the freezing temperature of the pitiful shower had only matched the ice in his blood, and in his heart.

Deep down, this was what he had always dreaded, what every person who didn't know their parents must secretly dread—that they would inadvertently fall in love with a blood relative. He looked at his reflection in the small square of mirror above the basin and hardly recognised himself.

His skin was ashen, his eyes like dark hollows, but suddenly in every line and plane of his face he could see the woman in the portrait downstairs laughing back at him. His mother.

Anna's mother.

Dio, it all slotted horribly, sickeningly into place. Snatches of his conversation with Sir William yesterday echoed around his head.

'*...the damage was already done...*'

Gripping the sides of the basin with both hands, Angelo braced his arms and bent his head, waiting for the wave of nausea to pass, wondering what to tell Anna. *Gesù*, he was blighted. Jinxed.

Cursed.

And now he had brought his poison into her life, infecting her with the blackness that had always shadowed him, like an indelible stain on his soul.

He couldn't tell her. This was a burden he would bear alone.

Anna stood at the window, looking down at the familiar view without seeing it. Her head throbbed with dull pain as self-reproach and recrimination chased themselves around her brain in sickening circles.

She had said the L-word.

How could she have been so bloody, bloody *stupid*?

Right from the beginning she had thrown herself at him in one humiliating episode after another, and he had never given her any reason to think the tumult of emotions he aroused in her was in any way reciprocated.

Well, maybe in *one* way, she thought, remembering the ferocity of his passion when he had caught her pole-dancing. But he had also never made any bones about the fact that sex was one of the many currencies he dealt in. He had many women.

But he didn't sleep *with them!* she thought in anguish. *That was what had made her reckless. The intimacy they had shared last night in the long dark hours he had lain beside her was what had deluded her!*

In her desolation she pressed her palms against the window-panes, the reflection of her own dark, haunted eyes staring back at her from the pale blur of her face. Behind her, she heard the door open and whirled round to see Angelo. He was dressed and there was something about him that told her he was leaving. Something final that said that in every way that mattered he was already gone.

'You're going?'

He hardly glanced at her as he spoke and his voice was cool and impersonal.

'Yes. I've got meetings this afternoon. I should have left last night really.'

'I'm sorry.' Her voice was very small. 'That was my fault.'

He gave an impatient sigh. 'Don't be silly; you couldn't help it.' He was looking around the room restlessly, as if he was just dying to be off. Anna felt her heart wither and die, her pride along with it as everything in her demanded that she throw herself at his feet and beg him not to go.

'Angelo—' she began desperately as tears surged into her eyes. 'I'm sorry, I'm so sorry. I was stupid to say that, but I wasn't being serious. I know I shouldn't have—'

He stopped her with a dismissive wave of his hand. 'Look, Anna, it doesn't really matter what you said. This was never going to come to anything, was it?' He gave a short, mirthless laugh, as if trying to emphasise the outrageousness of the idea that they could be together. 'I guess I just realised that it's all going a bit too far now. I shouldn't lead you on like this. I'm not right for you—'

'That's not true!' She was wringing her hands in a classic, clichéd gesture of distress but couldn't stop her cold fingers from twisting around each other, squeezing until the bones ached.

'Just *listen*!' It was almost a roar and she felt the blood drain from her face until she thought she might faint. '*You're* not right for me. It's not going to happen, Anna. I have a…a life and other…commitments, and I was wrong to stay here last night…'

His voice almost cracked. *Gesù, Gesù*, he had to stay strong.

'Other commitments?' she whispered, her face a mask of pain. He couldn't look at her. 'You mean you have someone else?'

'I'm sorry,' he said tonelessly and shrugged, thrusting his hands deep into his pockets as a physical restraint against the need to go to her and hold her. 'It's better that I leave now. Please don't come down.'

He didn't look back.

Downstairs, he strode along the passageway to the library where he had talked to Anna's father last night. The room was empty this morning, the fire cold, but the portrait above it was as warm and glowing as he remembered.

So that was the thing that had snagged in his brain. The earrings. In the picture they were little more than a smudge of crimson and blue-white oil, not easily identifiable, but now he knew he could recognize them all too clearly. Just as he could recognize his own eyes smiling back at him from Lisette Delafield's portrait.

He stood before it for just a few seconds, then turned on his heel and strode back towards the door.

He could hardly think straight to do the necessary pre-flight checks on the helicopter, he was so distracted by the idea of Anna looking out of one of the many blank windows that lined the front of the great barren house. He had a sudden vision of her like a princess abandoned in a tower, left to her fate. Cursed.

Cursed by me, he thought despairingly.

All the peace he had felt in the dark hours of the night had deserted him. There was no hope for him now—she had been his only chance of salvation, and now there was nothing standing between him and an eternity of aloneness.

The fires of hell seemed positively inviting by comparison.

CHAPTER FOURTEEN

LEAVING the warmth of Fliss's plush office at Arundel-Ducasse, Anna pulled her long black coat more tightly around her and put her head down against the wind. London in October was particularly bleak. But then, she thought, walking quickly along the crowded pavement towards the tube, she could have been lying on a beach in the Bahamas and it wouldn't have made any difference. Everywhere felt bleak when your heart had been hacked to bits with a pickaxe.

People said that time was supposed to be a great healer. Well, in Anna's opinion, time was doing a pretty rubbish job. It had been five interminably hideous weeks since Angelo had left, and her heart was definitely still on the critical list and showing no sign of recovery. She still cried herself to sleep every night, she still cried herself awake every morning, she still cried over songs on the radio and langoustines in the window of the fishmongers near Fliss's flat.

Fliss was making a very brave and very noble attempt at trying to remind her that her life wasn't over but, despite her best efforts, Anna wasn't convinced. Tired of leaving messages on Anna's voicemail, Fliss had appeared at Ifford one Saturday, two weeks after Angelo had gone, and found a pale, thin ghost of her former friend. Persuading Anna to take off Angelo's shirt and get dressed into some proper clothes had been the biggest hurdle:

after that, getting her to agree to come and stay in Fliss's flat in London, helping her find a part-time job in one of the trendy delis nearby and even getting her to eat occasionally had been relatively easy. Anna had simply submitted.

But recently even that numb submission had been shattered by two letters, forwarded from Ifford, from Angelo's firm of solicitors.

It had been the cold, impersonal tone that had upset her more than anything—until she thought of the implications behind it, and then that made the cold, impersonal tone seem like the least of her worries.

Our client regrets the breakdown of the relationship between himself and Lady Roseanna Delafield, but requires confirmation from a medical professional that Lady Delafield has not conceived a child as a result of the relationship. We regret the personal and sensitive nature of this request, but would appreciate your co-operation.

The excessive courtesy veiled the lethal, steel-tipped message. Really, she would rather he had just sent a scrawled note saying, *I'm really desperate never to have anything to do with you again, so please help me out by letting me know you have no further hold on me.* She would have respected him more.

Bloody hell, she thought bitterly, stumbling a little as her vision was blurred by another deluge of tears. Even thinking about it was enough to push her back into the swamp of her own misery. One day she'd simply sink without trace beneath the murky waters, like Alice in Wonderland, and—

Head down, she didn't see the face of the person she bumped into, only his elegant handmade shoes.

'Sorry, I wasn't—'

'What the—? *Gesù*, Anna!'

White-faced, she backed off, slightly winded by the force of her collision with the tall blond stranger in the dark suit, and shocked to the core by the realization it was no stranger. The crowd eddied around and between them, forcing them apart for a moment. He reached out to grab her arm, but she was too quick for him.

'Don't touch me!'

For a moment she thought she saw a flicker of emotion in the narrow blue eyes she remembered so perfectly, but when she looked again she realised she'd imagined it. They were as hard and cold as icebergs.

'I need to talk to you,' he said through gritted teeth, as if he was only hanging on to his temper by a thread, 'so don't even think of running away.'

'What? Like *you* did at Ifford?' she retorted, her eyes blazing at him.

He steadied himself, managed to produce a sardonic smile. 'I apologized for that at the time. And explained. I'm sure we can both be grown-up about it now.'

Anna looked down at the damp, leaf-strewn pavement and shook her head in disbelief. 'Oh, right,' she said sadly. 'That's what the solicitor's letters are about, is it? That's how *grown-ups* behave. Silly me. I'm just so immature.'

'You haven't replied.'

She looked up at him, feeling the wrenching pain in her poor, wounded heart as she did so. A little of the golden beach-boy glow he had had on the yacht had faded and he looked harder. Older. But still lethally handsome.

'No, Angelo, I haven't,' she said slowly. 'And I suppose it's only fair to warn you that I have no intention of doing so. You're a businessman, after all, so you might like to consider whether it's worth accumulating further legal fees when—ouch!'

He managed to get hold of her arm this time, his fingers burning her flesh through the layers of her clothes.

'I need an answer, Anna.'

'Why?' she spat, wrenching herself free of his grasp and backing away from him. 'Because you need to be in control? Well, you forfeited your right to control me when you left that morning. End of story. Goodbye, Angelo.'

She swung round and strode blindly down the busy street, grateful for the press of bodies around her, separating her from him and preventing her from rushing back and throwing her arms around him. She reached the tube station and was carried along in the flow of people going down the stairs when she was suddenly aware of a commotion behind her as someone pushed their way through.

She didn't have to turn round to know who it was. Of course he wouldn't be able to let her have the last word. The next moment he was standing in front of her, blocking her way, his broad shoulders like a sea wall against the tide of people.

'Nice try. But when I say I want to talk to you, I mean it.' He gave her a wintry smile. 'End of story.'

She looked at him, taking in the faultless tailoring of his dark wool suit, the snowy perfection of his white shirt, all of which emphasised his chilling beauty. In the dingy light of the underground tunnel his magnificence was utterly incongruous. She gave a slightly hysterical laugh.

'You really get to see how the other half lives when you're with me, don't you, Angelo? Hippy beach parties, squalid country houses, and now the sordid reality of the public transport system. Stick around—who knows what might be next on the itinerary?'

His face was like ice. 'Don't forget where I came from, Anna. I've slept in underground stations before now, so having a conversation here is no problem, I can assure you. Especially as it won't take long.'

'No. It won't. Because I have nothing to say.'

She looked up at him defiantly, her jaw set against the sob that was rising in her throat. He straightened up, half-turning away from her, and for a moment, just for a fraction of a second, caught a look of haunting despair in his face.

'Please. Anna. Just tell me. There's a risk, we both know that. Tell me you're not pregnant!'

She sighed, feeling the fight go out of her, and looked up at him with huge, troubled eyes. 'Why, Angelo? What would it matter to you? I'd never ask anything of you. I don't want your money.'

Angelo felt the barbed wire band around his heart twist and tighten and braced himself against the familiar pain. 'I just need to know. For personal reasons.'

She bent her head. Her voice was so quiet that he had to lean towards her to hear it, which meant he could smell her wonderful dark scent.

'You said you had…other commitments. Are you getting married? Is that it?'

The crowd were pushing past them to the platform and in the midst of all the people she looked so fragile that he wanted to push everyone else back from her and make a space for her in the circle of his arms. Instead he tipped his head back and breathed in deeply.

Forgive me.

'Yes,' he said curtly. 'Yes, that's it. I'd like everything… sorted…first. I think it's only fair that there's no danger of anything that happened in my past interfering with… our…future.'

He saw the top of her dark head move up and down as she nodded. Sliding her hands into the pockets of her long black coat, she hunched her shoulders and started to move forwards. He fell into step beside her and, glancing down, saw that tears were coursing down her cheeks.

Gesù. Benedetto Gesù. Each tear was like the lash of the torturer's whip. And he absorbed the blows without complaint because he knew he deserved them.

'I'm sorry, Anna.' Pitifully inadequate. But better than nothing.

She gave a bleak smile. 'The thing is, it doesn't really make any difference if I am pregnant or not. Because, you see, Angelo, I'm afraid that I would never, ever in a million years consider terminating a baby because it wasn't convenient or it didn't fit in with your plans. I'm surprised you'd even want me to, considering your past.' They had reached the platform and her face in the harsh fluorescent strip lighting was pale grey. A gust of air lifted her hair from her face and he could see the last traces of pink, like the fading rays of sunset. He felt the darkness closing in around him, sealing him off from the rest of humanity with his guilt and his shame and his bitterness.

'What do you mean, my "past"?'

Her voice was oddly apologetic. 'Your mother. She must have been alone, terrified, *devastated*, to do what she did with you, but she still gave you the opportunity of a life. I hope that in the same situation I'd be brave enough to do the same thing.'

He stared straight ahead at the grimy tiled wall, his jaw clenched, not trusting himself to blink.

Anna couldn't stop herself from gazing up at him. He looked like a tortured angel. Fliss kept telling her that anger was the only way to get through the pain, but as she looked at him she could find nothing inside her but love.

There was another gust of warm stale air and a surge of bodies signalling the arrival of the train. Pressed into him in the crush, she said fiercely, 'If I was pregnant, nothing would stop me having the baby. Keeping it. And loving it like I love you.'

And then, head down, she slipped past him into the crowd. He spun round, searching for her, feeling that he'd been kicked brutally in the guts. He saw her standing by the doors of the train and strode towards her.

'*Dio*, Anna! You don't understand...' His voice was harsh. Raw. 'You don't *know*!'

'I do. I'm adopted too.' She stepped into the carriage and looked back at him, smiling wanly through her tears. 'And, believe me, at the moment it doesn't feel like it, but generally I'm glad I'm alive.'

She stood back as the doors started to close, her eyes searching his face. He looked ashen. Stunned.

'I'm not pregnant. So—there you are. Go and be happy.'

And in just a few seconds the platform had become quiet and almost empty as the train disappeared into the darkness of the tunnel. Angelo stumbled backwards, leaning against the wall for support, fighting for breath.

I'm adopted too.

The implications filled his brain, too big, too wonderful to be easily comprehended. That was what she'd said, wasn't it? Meaning that Lisette Delafield wasn't her natural mother? That there was no blood tie between them?

Incredulously he rubbed his hands over his face, then stood up and began to walk quickly in the direction of the exit, back up towards the light. His mind raced. He felt like a prisoner who, having been kept for five long weeks in solitary confinement in the pitch blackness, was suddenly thrust back out into the open and had no idea which way to go.

He didn't know where Anna had gone, where she was living, how to find her. Pushing both hands into his hair, he gritted his teeth and tried to focus. It was possible that her father would help him, but he had no telephone number for Ifford Park and his jet was waiting to fly him back to France tonight.

And then, with a flash of hope, he remembered Arundel-Ducasse. He had been on his way to a meeting there when he had bumped into her, and since they had dealt with the sale of the château they would surely have a contact number.

His pace quickened until he was almost running, trying to suppress the terrible weight of hope that was crushing his chest. He could have misheard. Misunderstood.

He had spent the last five weeks in a state of frozen numbness. As a small boy in the orphanage, he used to dream of the day when he would find his natural mother, but as he had grown older he had ruthlessly repressed his curiosity. How cruel then that he should discover Lisette—unsought, unwanted—and have to give up Anna as a consequence. Part of him had railed against the injustice, wishing he could not have seen the earring, wishing she had not chosen to leave the other half of the pair with him, wishing he had never known...

But then the consequences could have been dire, the curse of his own blighted life visited on the children he and Anna might have.

And that was when the real torment had begun. Night after harrowing night of lying awake, wondering...torturing himself. Instructing his solicitors to contact her had been the least personal, most brutal way of trying to extract an answer from her, but he had known the hurt it would cause her. From the depths of his own pain he'd ached for her, but had recognized that making her hate him was the best possible course of action, the one most likely to encourage her to end the pregnancy, should that be necessary.

He had, of course, not reckoned on her courage, her sensitivity, her capacity for love.

Or her own experience of adoption.

Racing up the steps to the Arundel-Ducasse office, he paused at the top with his hand on the door, breathing fast, and then pushed it open.

'Can I help you, sir?' enquired the girl at the desk at the front of the office, looking up at him with a polite smile. The smile faded slightly as she added, with a barely distinguishable acid tone, 'Oh. Signor Emiliani.'

His gaze flickered over the little sign on her desk, on which her name was printed, and his face broke into a grim smile.

'Yes, Ms Hanson-Brooks, I think you can. Or may I call you Felicity?'

* * *

Fliss left the office early and hailed a taxi on the street outside. She had actually made a resolution to be less extravagant and had given up taxis, lunch-hour trips to Bond Street and champagne on weekdays, but hell, this had to qualify as Exceptional Circumstances.

Thrusting two twenty pound notes at the driver as he pulled up outside her flat, she slammed the door and ran up the path without waiting for the change. Throwing open the front door into the communal hallway, she clattered up the stairs as fast as her office heels would allow, unable to stop a huge giveaway grin from spreading across her face.

Finally she flung open the door to her own flat.

'Anna! Anna, just guess what? *Guess* who I've spent the afternoon with?'

But her voice echoed around the dark flat, dissolving into the thick silence. She didn't have to read the note on the kitchen worktop to know that Anna had left.

Darling Fliss
Am taking my misery away for a while. Sorry for being such awful company for the last few weeks and thanks for everything.
Anna. xx

Fliss swore succinctly. She wasn't going to enjoy breaking the news to Angelo.

CHAPTER FIFTEEN

'AND so the prince and the princess were married, and they all lived happily ever after…'

Anna shut the book and looked down at the small head nestled against her. 'And now it's time to go to sleep. Did you like that story, Suzette?' she asked, lifting the little girl into her narrow bed and tucking the covers around her.

Suzette nodded, her dark eyes shining. '*Oui.* I love the bit where they get married. Her dress is so beautiful. I'll have a dress like that when I get married.'

Anna smiled, feeling the familiar lump in her throat. 'I'm sure you will, *chérie.* And you'll have flowers in your hair and a big bouquet of roses and lilies… And you'll look even more beautiful than the princess in the picture.'

'*Oui.*' Slipping her thumb contentedly into her mouth, the little girl settled down beneath the covers and Anna bent to kiss the top of her head. The delicate sense of peace she had found during the last month at the convent and as a volunteer helper in its children's home had come as a surprise to her. In the early days when she had first arrived there she had wondered how she would survive, but she had. And slowly she had begun to feel ready to face the rest of her life again.

But it was time to leave now. In her one hurried, panicked phone call to Fliss on the night she'd arrived she had told her she was taking one month away. One month in which she couldn't be contacted, couldn't be tempted to make any contact with home. She remembered how Fliss had tried to stop her, had tried to interrupt, but she knew that if she listened she would give in, and sobbing, she had apologized and cut the call. The kindly nun who had taken her in had simply sat in benevolent silence as she'd cried.

So now that month had come to an end. In the outside world it was nearly Christmas, and Anna tried to picture crowds of shoppers and hot, frantic department stores. The thought filled her with horror and she would have liked to stay where she was—safe in the quiet and simple routines of the convent. But she was growing too fond of the children, and for their sakes that wasn't a good idea.

She stopped in the doorway, looking back at Suzette. 'Sweet dreams.'

'Anna?' Suzette murmured. 'Tomorrow can we have that story again?'

Anna smiled sadly. 'I'm sure you can, darling. Maybe Lily will read it to you.'

'*Non.* Want you.'

'I'm leaving tomorrow, sweetheart, remember?' she said with infinite gentleness.

There was a little pause. 'Oh. Yes,' Suzette said in a very small voice. And then she turned over and faced the wall.

Anna's scarred heart turned over too. She longed to go back and hold the little girl, who had already learned that no one in life was to be relied on. But what comfort could she offer?

After all, it was pretty much the truth.

Later, sitting at the window in her bare, cell-like room, she looked out over the tree-tops towards the château as she had done every night since she had been here.

When she had first left Fliss's flat she had no idea where she was going, only that she had to get away. Seeing Angelo like that, finding out that he was to be married, had been agony almost beyond endurance. She had tried to believe in the time after he had left her so suddenly at Ifford Park that the scars from his difficult past ran too deep and that he was simply incapable of love, but to find out that he was in love with someone else was unbearable. And she had found herself drawn back to the place where she had always felt safest.

The château.

It had been easy to get a seat on a flight for Nice that evening, and it was only as she'd stepped out of the familiar airport building and got into a taxi that she'd realised how stupid she was being. The château was sold—she knew that, but it would also be exactly where Fliss would think to look for her, and then she might contact Angelo, and...

She had pictured him pulling up in front of the château and getting out of the car. Leaning back in to say to the woman who waited in the passenger seat, *Sorry about this,* tesoro. *She's a bit unhinged...*

'Where to, *mademoiselle*?' the taxi driver had asked.

'The convent near to Belle-Eden.'

'Sacre Coeur? *Bon.*'

And that was how she had ended up coming home—to her first and unremembered home: the place where she had lived as a tiny baby before Sir William and Lisette had taken her. Until then it was the last place she could have imagined coming to, but something had changed that afternoon on that dingy station platform. From the wreckage of her future she had managed at least to salvage something worthwhile about her past, which, she reflected sadly, was completely the wrong way round to do things. But fairly typical of her.

She'd said it. *I'm adopted.*

No one had laughed. No one had sneered. No one had moved away from her in the carriage, even though most of them must have heard. To be perfectly honest, there hadn't been much room to move away, but no one had tried. Somehow saying it like that had been a relief, and had planted in her head the seed of the idea which had brought her here.

She had used to come with her mother when she was very small, she remembered, no more than five or six. Looking back, she thought her mother had probably brought her back to maintain contact with the nuns who had looked after her as a baby and arranged her adoption, and then the visits had stopped when she had grown old enough to ask questions.

The shame. That was where the shame had begun.

But it was over now. For the first time ever, she felt at peace with herself.

OK, so everything else about her life was like the aftermath of an earthquake and her heart was lost in the rubble, but at least she knew who she was.

Roseanna Delafield, Spinster of this Parish.

Great. Just great.

The nuns did not encourage emotional goodbyes. People came and went, and Anna had been just one of a constant trickle of the lost and the lonely and the broken-hearted through the small number of guest rooms at the convent. They had accepted her departure with the same serene impassivity as they had accepted her arrival, giving her a bunch of late flowering roses and anemones from the walled garden and wishing her well.

Getting into the waiting taxi, she took the mobile out of her bag for the first time in a month and turned it on. Without even checking her messages, she dialled Fliss's work number.

'Good morning, Arundel-Ducasse, Felicity speaking. How may—'

'Fliss. It's me.'

'Anna. *Anna!* Where are you? *How* are you? Oh, my God— where have you been?'

'I'm OK. I'm just outside Cannes, but I'm coming home. But first I'm going to stop off at the château. I want to put some flowers on mum's grave and then—'

'You're going to the château? Now? Oh, God. OK, Anna, I have to go. Call me soon, d'you promise? Soon.'

The phone went dead and Anna was left staring out of the window as the car sped along the last familiar miles to the château. The landscape that she knew so well in its green, high summer glory looked different now, stripped of its lusciousness. It was stark, uncompromising, but somehow more honest.

To her surprise, the tall wrought iron gates of the château were open—she had expected them to be shut and locked—but even so she asked the taxi driver to stop at the foot of the drive so that she could approach on foot. She wasn't sure what she would find. A busy building site perhaps, crawling with earth-movers and men in hard hats? A brand-new, pristine-looking clinic, built around the old château, obscuring it so that it was barely recognizable?

Rounding the last corner of the drive, she felt her footsteps falter and a gasp of disbelief spring to her lips.

It was like stepping back in time.

The château looked the same as she remembered it when she was a child, when it had been clean and cared for and scrupulously maintained under Grandmère's watchful eye. The rotting woodwork had been repaired and repainted, broken pipes and missing slates replaced, clumps of moss and weeds removed from gutters and cracks in the masonry. The place gleamed.

Still carrying the flowers she had come to put on her mother's grave, she hesitated, wanting so much to go in, but hardly daring to hope…

With shaking hands, she took her keys from her bag and, stepping up to the front door, tried the largest and oldest one in the polished lock. He would have changed them…surely… He wouldn't risk…

It slid in. And turned.

And then she was standing in the hall and it was just as it must have been over a century before when her great-grandfather had first brought his new bride to the home he had built for her. The limestone floor had been cleaned and buffed to a soft sheen and the walls painted a soft duck-egg blue that exactly matched the colour of the silk that had rotted and decayed. And the whole space was imbued with that magical light from the dome above, like the shadows of birds of paradise flitting through sunlight.

Walking in a daze up the stairs, Anna trailed her fingers up the newly stripped and polished wooden banister. Any minute now she expected to wake up in her hard little bed at the convent and find she had dreamed all this—it was almost too wonderful to take in. Wandering into Grandmère's room a second later, she gave a gasp and had to grip the door-frame for support.

The furniture that had been sent to the auction house that day was back—the grand bed with its delicately gilded wicker head-board was made up with piles of pristine white linen pillows and bolsters, covered in a chalky pink silk eiderdown, just as if Grandmère were expected to come and slip between its sheets at any moment. The dressing table stood in its old position beneath the window, and the vast heavy mahogany wardrobe had been replaced against the wall beside the doorway.

But then the dream slipped inexorably into a nightmare and Anna's blood ran cold.

There, hanging up on the wardrobe, swathed in layers of protective tissue and polythene, was a dress. A long ivory dress.

A wedding dress.

She heard her own cry of anguish as it was wrenched from her throat, felt her hands fly to her mouth to stop the sobs that spilled out of her as the truth dawned.

Angelo's plans had changed. The château was not to be used as a clinic, but as his own home, the place where he and his bride would live together and raise their family.

They would get married from here. Just as she had always wanted to do.

For a moment she couldn't move. It was as if her brain, unable to deal with the horror of the situation, had simply shut down for a moment, leaving her immobilized in the centre of the room, unable to think what to do next. Outside, she was faintly aware of noises—of a car door slamming and feet crunching on gravel—and that broke the spell. Looking wildly around her, she made a run for the stairs as below the front door burst open.

Reaching the top of the staircase, she froze, her heart smashing against her ribs. Angelo was there, standing below in the hallway, just as she had first seen him. Just as she had remembered him a million times since, just as she had imagined him a thousand times before, as a little girl in her homemade wedding dress.

He looked up at her, his eyes blazing.

'Anna!'

'I know,' she whispered hoarsely. 'I'm sorry, I shouldn't be here. I'm going.'

'No!' he roared, racing up the stairs towards her. She shrank back, trembling violently, and, seeing her horrified reaction, he stopped abruptly.

'Please, Angelo—don't say anything. I'm getting myself together. The last month has been…good. Anything you say will only make it worse again. Please.'

She was pleading with him. Standing close, he could see the dark shadows of anguish beneath her beautiful dark eyes and it took all his self-restraint not to grab her and kiss them away. Instead he shoved his hands into his pockets.

'We have to talk, Anna. There's so much you don't know about.'

'No!' She almost shouted the word and her voice echoed around the walls and into the high dome above them, reproaching him with the hollow sound of her despair. 'Angelo—I've seen the wedding dress! I don't need to hear anything more!'

He gave a groan and raised his hands to his head. 'You saw it. I'm sorry—I wanted to speak to you first.'

'There's no need.' With a terrible gasping sob, she pushed past him and clattered down the stairs. 'You told me in London you were getting married, remember? It's not like I haven't had time to get used to the idea, but—' She stopped, grabbing hold of the banister for support and turning slowly back to look up at him. Her face was wet with tears. 'That doesn't mean I've got over it.'

Dizzying hope crashed through him. In his desperation to get things straight between them he'd forgotten he'd made up the line about getting married. She'd seen the dress and assumed it was for someone else... Oh, *Dio*...

'No,' he moaned. 'Oh, Anna, no... The dress... Did you not look at it properly?'

She let out a high, slightly hysterical laugh. 'Why? So I would be able to picture properly just how very beautiful your bride will be on your wedding day, Angelo? I think not. I think I'd prefer blissful ignorance and a bottle of vodka, if you don't mind.'

'Anna, come here.' His voice was heartbreakingly gentle.

'I can't.' Her mouth was quivering.

He sighed. 'OK, I'll come down to you.'

'No!' she cried. 'Don't, Angelo. Don't make it worse.'

She was like a frightened animal, he thought. One false move on his part and she would disappear into the undergrowth and he would have lost her for ever. Tension knotted in his chest, making it difficult to breathe properly. Maybe she was right. Maybe it was best that he said what he had to say now, while he wasn't distracted by her closeness. He had no idea how she would take it. When she found out he was Lisette's son she might never want to see him again.

'There's something I have to tell you, Anna. It might not be easy for you to hear.'

Oh, God, he's going to say she's pregnant! Anna's hands went to her ears. 'Angelo, please! I don't need to hear any more!'

His self-control snapped. 'Yes! Yes, you do! Just bloody listen to me, Anna!'

'*Why?* You've destroyed me already! Isn't that enough?'

He sat down heavily on to the stairs, dropping his head into his hands. 'Look, Anna, I left you at Ifford that day, not because of anything you did or said, but because of this.' He took a small, square box from his pocket and held it out to her. She closed her eyes.

'You were going to ask whoever she is to marry you,' she whispered brokenly.

'No!' He ground the word out through clenched teeth. 'Here.' He tossed the box down to her. 'Look at it.'

Warily she snapped it open and looked up at him uncomprehendingly. 'My pendant. I don't understand...'

'*Not* your pendant. The missing earring. Lisette's missing earring. I was left at a convent when I was a few hours old, wrapped in a cashmere shawl with *that* tucked into it.'

Her eyes were very wide, filled with alarm. 'My mother...?'

'Was my mother,' he said tonelessly. 'Apparently she had a brief relationship with someone else the summer she got engaged to your father and it seems I was the unwelcome result. I thought you were my sister. I couldn't believe what I'd done to you, and I just had to get away before I dragged you down into hell with me.

Silence settled in the majestic hallway as Anna looked down at the small arrangement of rubies and diamonds against the dark velvet. Disjointed thoughts swirled around her head as fragments of the last harrowing months came back to her, fitting together to give a picture of Angelo's suffering.

'That was why you wanted to know if I was pregnant,' she whispered.

'Yes.'

She caught the break in his voice. And looked up at him.

He wore the same expression of fierce determination she'd

seen on his face that day at the station, only this time, as she gazed at him, she caught the minute tremble of his beautiful mouth and understood its meaning. Her heart turned over.

'Oh, Angelo,' she breathed. 'I'm sorry…'

He stood up quickly and turned away from her, walking up the stairs out of view. Anna shut the box and slowly climbed the stairs after him, her mind dazed with a million thoughts and questions, all of which came back to one thought, one question.

She found him in her grandmother's room, standing at the window as he had on the day she had first met him. Outside, the winter's day was grey and misty and against it his blond head was like burnished gold. Hesitantly she walked towards him, still holding the flowers limply in one hand.

'Angelo? Why didn't you tell me?'

He didn't turn his head, but shook it slowly, hopelessly. 'And see you look at me with disgust? How could I?' In the darkness of the window-pane, she thought she saw the glimmer of tears on his face and she wanted so much to slide her arms around his waist and press her face against his back and hold him tightly.

But, of course, she couldn't. He wasn't hers to hold.

'It was my fault,' she said with a moan of anguish. 'If only I'd been more honest about myself instead of trying to hide who I was—that I was…adopted…none of this would ever have happened. It seems so *stupid*, but my parents had hidden it from me for so many years and it was as if it was something to be ashamed of. My father…it was so difficult for him, so humiliating, with the weight of all that family responsibility, to find he couldn't have children, and I guess I just took on *his* shame. *I* felt ashamed too, that I was the one who had broken that Delafield bloodline that stretched all the way back to the Norman sodding Conquest. I felt like an impostor, a fake. And then, that day at the station, I realised *none of that matters*. I *am* lucky…But—' Sobs choked her and for a moment she couldn't continue. Swallowing, taking deep gulps of air, she controlled herself enough to smile painfully through the tears and say, 'Typical me, I guess. I realized too late.'

Slowly he turned to face her. His face was brutally blank.

'Why?' he asked in a voice like gravel. 'Why too late?'

'The dress,' she said hopelessly, gesturing to where it hung on the wardrobe, swathed in protective layers. 'The wedding dress.'

'Look at it.'

Haltingly, hesitantly, she crossed the room. Placing the flowers carefully on the silk counterpane, she stood in front of the dress and, with shaking hands, she lifted the polythene, folding it back over the hanger. And then she stepped back.

Her hands flew to her mouth as more tears slid down her cheeks, unchecked. There, in exquisite thick ivory satin was a perfect recreation of the small ragged dress her mother had made for her. The details were all there—from the tight fitted bodice with the grosgrain ribbon across the bust, to the flared ballerina-length skirt with its delicious layers of net beneath, all expertly made in the most sumptuous fabric.

She couldn't speak.

In the mirrored door of the wardrobe she saw him watching her and the expression of tortured love on his face stole her breath and stopped her heart. The next moment he was standing in front of her, gently peeling her fingers from across her mouth and brushing her quivering lips with his thumbs as he cupped her face in his hands.

'It's yours. Everything's yours. The château, the furniture, the dress, everything.'

'You?'

'Oh, Anna...' he moaned softly. 'It goes without saying but, just to avoid any more confusion, I'm going to say it anyway. I'm yours. Everything I have is yours. I love you. And maybe you're too free-spirited to do anything as conventional and boring as getting married, and if you don't want to it won't matter, because

I'll go on loving you whatever, and you can wear that dress with your bare feet and dance on the beach in it for all I care…' He kissed her mouth, very intently. 'Just as long as I can be there. Always.'

'And what if I *want* to get married?'

'Then, please, marry me.' He smiled wearily. 'Marry me as soon as possible and put your poor friend Felicity out of her misery. She's been looking at bridesmaids' dresses ever since you went away and she's desperate to know what colour you'll let her have.'

And then she was laughing and crying and then his lips caught hers again and she was oblivious to everything else. It was a few moments before either of them realized that his mobile was ringing, and a few more before he tore his mouth from hers and answered it.

'Fliss. Yes, I'm with her now…' Smiling, his eyes flickered to Anna's, the clear blue smoky with love. 'Yes, I have asked her, actually,' he said dryly, and then frowned. 'Do you know, I don't think she's actually given me an answer yet…'

'Yes,' Anna whispered, looking into his eyes. Then she tipped back her head and yelled, 'Yes, yes, *yes!*'

Angelo raised an eyebrow. 'Did you get that? She said *yes*…'

REQUEST YOUR FREE BOOKS!

 HARLEQUIN *Presents*

2 FREE NOVELS PLUS 2 FREE GIFTS!

PASSION GUARANTEED SEDUCTION

YES! Please send me 2 FREE Harlequin Presents® novels and my 2 FREE gifts (gifts are worth about $10). After receiving them, if I don't wish to receive any more books, I can return the shipping statement marked "cancel". If I don't cancel, I will receive 6 brand-new novels every month and be billed just $4.05 per book in the U.S. or $4.74 per book in Canada, plus 25¢ shipping and handling per book and applicable taxes, if any*. That's a savings of close to 15% off the cover price! I understand that accepting the 2 free books and gifts places me under no obligation to buy anything. I can always return a shipment and cancel at any time. Even if I never buy another book, the two free books and gifts are mine to keep forever.

106 HDN ERRW 306 HDN ERRL

Name	(PLEASE PRINT)
Address	Apt. #
City	State/Prov.	Zip/Postal Code

Signature (if under 18, a parent or guardian must sign)

Mail to the Harlequin Reader Service:
IN U.S.A.: P.O. Box 1867, Buffalo, NY 14240-1867
IN CANADA: P.O. Box 609, Fort Erie, Ontario L2A 5X3

Not valid to current subscribers of Harlequin Presents books.

Want to try two free books from another line?
Call 1-800-873-8635 or visit www.morefreebooks.com.

* Terms and prices subject to change without notice. N.Y. residents add applicable sales tax. Canadian residents will be charged applicable provincial taxes and GST. Offer not valid in Quebec. This offer is limited to one order per household. All orders subject to approval. Credit or debit balances in a customer's account(s) may be offset by any other outstanding balance owed by or to the customer. Please allow 4 to 6 weeks for delivery. Offer available while quantities last.

Your Privacy: Harlequin Books is committed to protecting your privacy. Our Privacy Policy is available online at www.eHarlequin.com or upon request from the Reader Service. From time to time we make our lists of customers available to reputable third parties who may have a product or service of interest to you. If you would prefer we not share your name and address, please check here. ☐

HP08R

MEDITERRANEAN DOCTORS

Demanding, devoted and
drop-dead gorgeous—
These Latin doctors will
make your heart race!

Smolderingly sexy Mediterranean doctors

Saving lives by day…red-hot lovers by night

**Read these four Mediterranean Doctors stories
in this new collection by your favorite authors,
available in Presents EXTRA October 2008:**

THE SICILIAN DOCTOR'S MISTRESS
by SARAH MORGAN

THE ITALIAN COUNT'S BABY
by AMY ANDREWS

SPANISH DOCTOR, PREGNANT NURSE
by CAROL MARINELLI

THE SPANISH DOCTOR'S LOVE-CHILD
by KATE HARDY

▼ Silhouette®

SPECIAL EDITION™

FROM *NEW YORK TIMES* BESTSELLING AUTHOR

LINDA LAEL MILLER

A STONE CREEK CHRISTMAS

Veterinarian Olivia O'Ballivan finds the animals in Stone Creek playing Cupid between her and Tanner Quinn. Even Tanner's daughter, Sophie, is eager to play matchmaker. With everyone conspiring against them and the holiday season fast approaching, Tanner and Olivia may just get everything they want for Christmas after all!

Available December 2008
wherever books are sold.